DYKESCAPES

DYKESCAPES

edited by TINA PORTILLO

Boston: Alyson Publications, Inc.

"As Important as a Lamp" appeared in slightly different form as "Duck-ing/Dodging" in *Common Lives/Lesbian Lives*, no. 26 (Spring 1988).

"Cactus Love" appeared in slightly different form in *On Our Backs*, vol. 5, no. 4 (March–April 1989).

"Merry Christmas, Katherine" appeared in slightly different form in the *Arizona Literary Magazine* (1986 edition).

"The Revenge of Chunky Beef" appeared in slightly different form in *Sinister Wisdom*, no. 40 (1990).

"Robyn" appeared in slightly different form in the *Evergreen Chronicles: A Lesbian and Gay Literary Journal* (Winter 1989).

This is a paperback original from Alyson Publications, Inc.
40 Plympton St., Boston, Mass. 02118.
Distributed in England by GMP Publishers,
P.O. Box 247, London N17 9QR England.

First edition, first printing: June 1991

5 4 3 2 1

ISBN 1-55583-195-8

To all the young dykes
who want to write —
JUST DO IT.

CONTENTS

Introduction ix

Merry Christmas,
Katherine 3 *Ouida Crozier*

Natural bridges 19 *Pamela Gray*

One Sunday morning 29 *Shelley Anderson*

Smoke signals 36 *Jayne Relaford Brown*

Buzzard takes flight 44 *Ivy Burrowes*

Shubop's saga 56 *Wickie Stamps*

Cactus love 69 *Lee Lynch*

Teamwork 77 *Lucy Jane Bledsoe*

To Anna 95 *Elissa Goldberg*

A date with Deth 102 *Karen Barber*

Daddy's home 110 *Jessie Lynda Lasnover*

Saying good-bye 119 *Karen Dale Wolman*

As important as a lamp 131 *Carol Seajay*

Wood burning 137 *Kathleen M. Quinlan*

Unannounced 143 *Elaine J. Auerbach*

Robyn 156 *Nona M. Caspers*

The revenge of
Chunky Beef 163 *Emily A. Levy*

The contributors 173

INTRODUCTION

When I first started soliciting stories for this anthology, I sent notices to every journal I could find that was of any possible interest to writers. The results were slow in coming, but after several months stories began to pour in. My usual spare-time reading was put on hold while I spent weekends looking through hundreds of manuscripts. Occasionally this became pleasure reading — these selections I set aside for consideration. If I fell in love with a character or if a story brought forth a spontaneous grin or sniffle, it went into my "yes" pile, because as a lifelong reader, I believe that good fiction *must* produce some emotional reaction in the reader.

Naming this book was also tough. "Dyke" being my favorite tag for myself as a gay woman, that word simply *had* to appear somewhere in the title. After I discarded everything that has already been used, a title finally came to me that would not let go. The variegation of scenes, in their action and settings, brought to mind a series of different-colored landscapes; hence, the final title, *Dykescapes*.

Work by new writers is complemented by a gift from well-known author Lee Lynch, in the form of her story

"Cactus Love," a wonderful western about two senior lesbians who find each other and rediscover the joys of love and hot sex. In "Buzzard Takes Flight," Ivy Burrowes, who made her debut in Michael Nava's mystery anthology *Finale,* tells a sensitive story of the relationship between a fat dyke and her close friend.

Homophobia, as I see it, is the biggest issue plaguing the gay community. Therefore, I wanted to include stories that dealt with this subject creatively. Kathleen M. Quinlan portrays a heterosexual married woman who faces down her own homophobia in "Wood Burning." Through an "Unannounced" visitor, Elaine J. Auerbach relates how an older closeted lesbian, grieving over a late lover, is encouraged to let go, come out, and get on with her life. Jock dykes will have fun with Lucy Jane Bledsoe's little romp on and off the basketball court; her cast of characters, which includes an interracial couple, uses "Teamwork" to battle an overambitious homophobe in their midst.

Most touching of all the characters, for me, is Nona M. Caspers's "Robyn," a gay male PWA who is visited by his lesbian sibling as he lies on his hospital deathbed, in what may very well be their last encounter. Among other issue-oriented stories is "As Important as a Lamp," in which Carol Seajay gives us a woman's-eye view of a battered lesbian's courageous struggle to survive. Pamela Gray demonstrates to us how "Natural Bridges" can form between members of a family, as a son learns to be friends with both his "divorced" dyke mom and his new step-mom. In Ouida Crozier's "Merry Christmas, Katherine," we are treated to a glimpse of the budding romance between an older dyke professor and her 22-year-old former student.

Although Shelley Anderson does not deal directly with being gay in "One Sunday Morning," she gives a poignant account of a prepubescent baby dyke who is confronted with the issue of racism before she actually discovers her own sexuality. Another story whose theme is not blatantly lesbian is "Saying Good-bye" by Karen Dale Wolman, a tender tale of a simple yet genuine friendship between two young women whose unconditional love for each other is rare and inspiring.

Being who I am, I insisted on having controversy. In this volume you will find all kinds — from the separatist vegetarian incest survivor in Emily Levy's "The Revenge of Chunky Beef," to Wickie Stamps's equally hard-hitting S/M biker dykes with gay boyfriends in "Shubop's Saga."

Not enough has been written concerning what life is really like in women's detention centers. Jessie Lynda Lasnover deftly handles the subject with her realistic portrayal of sexy role-playing dyke inmates in "Daddy's Home." And there is humor here: I couldn't resist Karen Barber's "A Date with Deth," a snappy little thriller starring a gorgeous female Casanova.

In "Smoke Signals," Jayne Relaford Brown skillfully uses gender-blurring to detail the life of a youngster coping with having a mother who has been institutionalized for mental illness. Elissa Goldberg employs a unique vehicle — a letter from an older Jewish man "To Anna," his late wife — to bring us a heart-rending story dealing with lesbian issues.

Many people helped to make this anthology a reality. I want to express my sincere thanks to Sasha Alyson, for giving me this chance to tap some of the talent that is out there and gather these fine stories all together in one volume. I also want to thank Barbara Burg, Karen Mix, Candyce Rusk, and Schroeder Stribling, who volunteered to read manuscripts and thereby helped with the decision-making process; and Phyllis Cavanaugh, Lynne Yamaguchi Fletcher, Michelle Maihiot, Susan Reddy, Molly Ruggles, and Sue Willing, who all saved the day by reading more for me at the last minute. Many more thanks go to my co-workers at Alyson Publications, for their aid and for keeping their faith in me from the beginning to the end; Michael Nava, for his encouragement and helpful hints in the early days; Dianna ONeill, whose insight and energetic assistance was a boon; Jeffrey McMahan, for being so perceptive; Catherine Hopkins, for a *fabulous* book cover; my dear comrade Phyllis Cavanaugh, whose unwavering love and support was the morale booster I greatly needed at times; Darryl Pilcher, who kept me going by unwittingly acting as my pacemaker while simultaneously at work on his book; and everyone who helped in little and big ways whenever I asked them to. Most of all, my heartfelt gratitude goes to Mom and Dad, who had me reading years before I ever saw the inside of a schoolroom.

You have all played a necessary part in creating a collection that has something for everyone — whether female or male, gay or nongay, "correct" or "incorrect" — and is sure to stimulate as well as amuse.

Tina Portillo
April 1991

DYKESCAPES

MERRY CHRISTMAS, KATHERINE

OUIDA CROZIER

The buzzer sounded, jolting Katherine with its customary stridency and insistent message. She hated it, and hurried to respond before the clamor could jangle her nerves again.

With irritation, she swung the door back — she had been expecting a quiet evening at home, alone — then hesitated, surprised. "Well, Judy — hello," she said, her voice that mixture of irritation and surprise, with a question at the end. Deliberately, she neither moved aside nor invited the young woman in.

Judy stood on the stoop, in shadow. It was snowing softly behind her, and wet flakes clung to her coat and dark hair. "May I come in, Dr. Nikles?"

Katherine stepped aside, nursing her feeling of being intruded upon, aware of being dressed in gown and robe and slippers, her hair pinned back. She felt vulnerable, and resentful, at the invasion of her privacy. She did not take

3

well to unexpected, unannounced visits, whether from students or her peers. Few of her friends would have dared such an action. However, Judy was oblivious of this and walked right on into the living room. She seemed to catch herself in the act of inspecting things and turned, focusing on Katherine.

"I apologize for barging in like this," she began, her hazel eyes fixed on Katherine's. Kate noticed that the pupils were dilated and wondered if Judy were intoxicated — she had never thought of the young woman as a user. "But," Judy went on steadily, "I felt I *had* to talk to you, and—" She paused, dropping her eyes for a moment. "I was afraid that if I called first, you might say no." As she looked up again, she seemed suddenly shy.

"Yes," Katherine responded, "I probably would have said no." She waited, ungivingly, for the rest.

As if to restore her intent, Judy opened her coat, slipped out of it, and pulled off her scarf, stuffing it into one sleeve, then folded the coat inside out and laid it on a chair near the door. She turned to Katherine again, a mixture of fear and defiance on her face.

The expression touched Kate, reminding her of herself at Judy's age, and she relented a little. She looked pointedly at Judy's boots, wet with the snow.

"Well, you're here — you might as well take those off, too. I'll heat some water for something hot to drink." She went into the small kitchen, a smile playing around the corners of her mouth at the gratitude she had glimpsed in Judy's eyes as she had given permission to stay. "What would you like?" she called.

In stocking feet, Judy came through the swinging door. Kate noticed how, in the girl's wet hair, gold highlights glistened under the bright kitchen lights. Why am I thinking of her as a girl? she chided herself. She must be at least twenty-two by now. She reflected that in the perennial student garb of jeans and sweater, Judy didn't *look* at all like a girl. I must be getting old, Kate sighed inwardly.

Now that she was welcomed, Judy perused her surroundings more freely, while she murmured aloud. "Umm, I guess — I guess I'll have — well, uh, what do you have, Dr. Nikles?"

Kate laughed. "I have coffee and decaf, instant. I have caffeine teas — jasmine and pekoe — and I have herbal almond, and some of that 'Zinger' stuff." She waited while Judy finished her visual tour.

"Hmm. I guess jasmine tea, please. I seldom get to drink it and it's one of my favorites." Her voice, as usual, was just slightly breathy. Kate knew Judy smoked too much.

Katherine poured in silence, then handed Judy's cup to her. "Let's sit in here," she said, leading the way back into the living room. It was cozy with all the shades drawn and warmly lit — not a striking room, but a comfortable one, and one that reflected Katherine's personality. She had recently painted, and she liked the new ambience of the warm beige. The walls were hung with varied pictures in frames that displayed the natural wood: a poster of a Mojave girl, from an exhibit of early-American photography she had once attended; a watercolor done by a friend from a photo of her own of shrimpers in harbor; a miniature of a Renaissance painting of a woman in a richly blue gown; a David Hamilton nude. Plants, records, and books made up most of the rest of the contents of the room. Kate chose her favorite, much-used chair and sipped her decaf while Judy stood indecisively eyeing a nondescript couch some distance from where Katherine now reposed. Just as she was about to surrender herself to it, she spied a large pillow in the corner.

"May I use that to sit on?" she asked hopefully, moving toward it.

Kate nodded, beginning to feel exasperated. Her quiet evening was ticking away, forever lost to her.

Judy placed the pillow directly in front of Katherine, about four feet away, and settled herself on it. She stared into the tea, as if she were reading something of great importance in the dried blossoms floating there. Just as Katherine drew breath to break the silence, Judy cleared her throat to speak. She addressed the cup of tea, but the words, obviously, were meant for Katherine.

"Dr. Nikles, I came here tonight because I need to be honest with you about something."

Oh lord, Kate thought. Here it comes, another student confession about some perceived transgression.

"Dr. Nikles," Judy repeated, lifting her head, her dark pupils striking directly into Kate's eyes, "I ... am in love with you."

There was a dead silence in the room as two pairs of eyes locked, vision wavering and dimming, and two hearts pounded — one in astonishment, the other with fear and passion. One could have heard the snow fall, had anyone been listening.

Oh, my god! thought Kate. What *can* she be saying? A sick feeling, familiar, but unexperienced in many years, washed over her as she sat staring at the girl whose eyes remained locked on hers. And with that wave came the unbidden thought, How could she know? How could she *possibly* know?

She drew breath. "Judy," she began softly.

"Dr. Nikles, please — listen to what I have to say."

"Judy," Kate tried again.

Judy put down her cup and raised herself on her knees. Now she was all of two feet away, her face just slightly below Katherine's line of vision. She rested on her heels, her hands gripping her thighs as if for strength — or control. I wonder which, Kate mused.

"This is something I have not come to lightly — something it has taken me a long time to acknowledge and

accept — something I had to work at coming to you with."
She paused, and Katherine tried again.

"But, Judy—"

"Please!" Judy interrupted, fixing her with a look. "This is not high school, and although you have been my instructor and I your student, I am an adult and can freely make my own choices. I *know* what I am about." She paused again, and this time Kate thought better of trying to stop her. "I *am* in love with you — you are always somewhere in the back of my awareness, a comforting presence, an exciting and tantalizing *ab*sence. I find myself drafting letters and poems to you when I'm changing classes, or doing laundry, or in the shower — I can't stop thinking about you." Her voice had steadied and quieted as she had gone on, more sure now of being allowed her say. Her eyes, bright and intense with passion, softened, and she seemed to turn inward, attending to herself and what she had to express. She knew Katherine was not going to get up and walk away.

In fact, Kate found herself rigidly holding her cup and considered the fact that it was not in pieces on the floor a remarkable example of her self-possession. As she listened to the growing surety in Judy's voice, she put the cup aside and willed herself to relax, sit back, and hear the young woman out. She folded her arms loosely across herself, again all too aware of her rather intimate apparel. As Judy's focus softened and became more vague, she found herself flicking her own eyes over Judy, noting the long, graceful fingers gripping ample thighs, allowing herself to see for the first time, really, the full breasts, and thinking, Yes, she *is* a young *woman*.

Kate knew, within herself, that she had been attracted to this young woman from the first day she had set eyes on her, nearly a year ago. Judy Baltierra, second from the top on her alphabetic roster, had walked into Katherine's English 306, Twentieth-Century American Writers, class, and sat right in front of her. From then on, Kate had had a growing struggle to dampen her awareness of Judy, to maintain the usual student-teacher relationship, to, eventually, hide her feelings from herself. For having Judy in her class that semester had been mixed agony and pleasure: Judy was an excellent student, incisive and creative, with a flare for language and literature — a delight to any teacher — and yet, as the weeks had gone by, Katherine's initial attraction had strengthened to where she had felt it necessary to suppress her excitement at seeing Judy on campus, at hearing her voice on the phone when she called with questions about assignments, at watching her walk through the door at the beginning of every class. All in all, it had been with relief when the end of the term had come and she had known that she would not see Judy during the summer.

The long hot months had dragged by and Kate had convinced herself that she had forgotten about the young woman with the auburn hair and slightly freckled nose, who was within a fraction of Kate's own height, but of a heavier build. Not beautiful by today's standards, Kate had once thought, likening her to a Rubens painting, but very attractive, with thick lashes over hazel eyes which seemed always to have the spark of mischief flickering in them, and that wonderful, hearty laugh which could bring a smile and her own answering laughter to Kate. In Kate's eyes, Judy was beautiful, and Kate knew she was connected to her somewhere down around her navel.

Suddenly she was aware that Judy was speaking directly to her again, seeking her with her gold-flecked eyes. She pulled herself back to the present, to what Judy was saying.

"I thought, last spring, that when I was out of your class and wouldn't see you any more, I would get over my feelings about you. And I did manage to engross myself in my summer internship.

8

"But when I returned to campus in August to register for fall classes, it all came back, stronger than ever, and I knew that *somehow* I had to deal with all of this, not run away — that I couldn't pretend to myself that I could 'get over' you, any more." Her eyes were focused and intent again, and Kate hung now on Judy's every word, mesmerized. "I decided to start seeing a counselor and talk about all this—"

Kate gasped, involuntarily.

"It's okay, I'm not seeing anyone connected with school," she hastened to assure.

Kate felt herself breathe again. Thank god, thank god she's mature enough to recognize what *that* could've meant!

Judy went on. "You would have no reason to know this, Dr. Nikles, but I've known since I was about twelve or thirteen that I'm gay — I just sort of worked it all out for myself. So that wasn't the issue — the issue was what I was going to do about my feelings for you." She paused again, picked up her cup, and drank the rest of what Kate thought must have been, by now, piss-cold tea. Then she shifted and sank down on the pillow again, somehow managing to scoot it closer to Katherine as she did.

Kate felt trapped — she could not shift or draw back any further, and did not know that she cared to hear any more about Judy's counseling, either. She gambled. "More tea?" she said and stood up, feeling safer.

Judy looked up at her, reproach warring with sympathy on her face. Kate guessed Judy knew that she was having her own struggles just now. Judy dropped her gaze after a moment, mumbling, "No, thank you," as Kate edged toward the door.

"I believe I will," she tossed over her shoulder, praying as she went that Judy wouldn't follow her. In the relative privacy of the kitchen, she allowed herself to experience her own agitation, leaning against the bar and putting her head down for a moment. She tried to breathe easily and relax while the water heated. Then she retreated to the bathroom. As she washed her hands, she examined herself in the mirror, attempting to ascertain that what she was wearing was neither suggestive nor seductive. She debated changing, or taking her hair down, but knew that was just too absurd. What has happened has had nothing to do with nightclothes! she told herself, gazing ruefully at her reflection.

When she returned, she noticed that Judy had moved back a little, but she contrived to sit sideways in the chair anyway, trying to put yet more space between them. She waited for Judy to begin again, knowing that she would take up the conversation unasked.

Judy toyed with a loose thread on the pillow before she began to speak, but when she did, her full attention was centered on Katherine. Kate found it very disconcerting. "So, I've spent the past two and a half months looking at my feelings about you and have come to some important awarenesses."

When she paused, Katherine interjected a diverting question. "Who've you been seeing?" she flung over her coffee cup.

Judy shot back a look that said, I'm not falling for *that* one! "Karen Wise," she replied sharply. Then, amending carelessly, "Know her?"

Kate fancied that she had paled noticeably. "Yes," she murmured, sipping her decaf. If Judy only knew what Kate knew! Kate and Karen had once been lovers — a long time ago, but still ... She was relieved that Judy seemed to have paid very little attention to her reply — she was gathering herself to move on. How intent she is! Kate thought.

"Well, I found out that *some*" — she emphasized it heavily — "of my stuff about you has to do with my mother."

Kate flinched. Her mother! Jesus Christ, her *mother?* We're only fifteen years apart! What was a fifteen-year difference when *I* was Judy's age? she asked herself, and

10

could not remember. She was amazed that she seemed to convey a sense of calmness to Judy when inwardly she was feeling as if she were losing it.

"But," Judy emphasized further, and then her voice softened again, "I also got quite clear that I love you." That direct gaze — which Kate had found occasionally unnerving from the first row of a classroom — was fixed on her again, and Kate felt impelled to respond.

"Judy," she broached, half expecting to be cut off again, "Judy, do you even *begin* to realize what you're saying?" She acknowledged the look on Judy's face with a change of direction. "All right, you do realize — at least *some* of what you're saying. But, Judy, you hardly know me. How can you possibly think you're in love with me? Judy—" She broke off, at a loss for words in the face of the determined expression the other woman wore.

They sat and stared at one another for a moment, Judy with the coolness of clarity and resolve after puzzling through a confusion, Katherine with a blend of incredulity and pleading on her face and in her eyes. Abruptly, but not hurriedly, Judy got to her knees again, only this time she was inches away from where Katherine sat shrinking into her chair.

"Katherine," she said in a near whisper, "I want you. I love you and I want you, and that is that." Her eyes bored into Katherine's and Kate realized that the pupil dilation she had observed earlier had nothing to do with drugs — it was quite simply due to passion. She felt her heart leap into her throat and knew she must get away. But how? Judy's hands were on the arms of her chair, her body blocking escape.

She sat forward, intending to push past the other woman if necessary, but Judy gave way with one arm. Katherine struggled to her feet and turned to Judy, who remained half crouched in front of the chair. "Judy, please," she began again. "You can't possibly think that I could be involved with you—" She took another tack. "What does Karen think of all this?" She knew she was grabbing at straws, but she felt she had to try to regain her space and her composure. How could I have let myself in for this? she questioned silently.

Judy stood and faced her squarely from a foot away. "Karen thinks I need to work this out with you, on my own, and in person — which is why I'm here tonight," she added, moving a bit closer.

Kate found herself turning and stepping away, but as she did so she decided she was not going to give any further ground. She sighed and drew herself into her center. "All right, Judy, what if I said I am not interested in you — not interested in being involved with you?"

Judy stepped toward her again, but less aggressively. "I think it would be a lie, Katherine," she replied quietly, her voice holding a quality that was almost a sadness.

Katherine met her look, felt herself being searched, knew the truth lay just below the surface. "Judy, you are — I am — there are fifteen *years* between us!" Judy made no reply, merely continued her unwavering appraisal. Katherine stepped toward her, but she gave no ground either.

"Judy, we can't — it just won't work. There are too many differences."

"How can you know that without trying?" came the even reply.

As Kate heard the response to her question, she found her hands resting on the other woman's shoulders and wondered how they got there, but she did not withdraw. Instead, she gripped harder, as if by the pressure of her hands she could force some awareness, or acceptance. "What makes you think I could love you, or want to be with you?" She tried to be gentle with her words. Nonetheless, she saw Judy flinch.

12

"You've loved other women," Judy said softly, neither a statement nor a question, but a tentative framing of reality.

Katherine nodded, having long ago given up any thought of pretense. "Yes, I have," she acknowledged quietly, "but that doesn't mean—" She broke off as Judy's hands found her shoulders and Judy stepped forward so that they were nearly touching. Kate could feel the space between them reverberating. Her heart was pounding madly in her chest and she could hear a roaring in her ears. Dear god, she thought, if she doesn't stop—

Judy kissed her and Kate's heart stopped. She sucked in air as Judy released her, her hands involuntarily tightening on the other's shoulders. "Oh, Judy," she rasped, her throat aching and throbbing with suppressed words and feelings. Again their eyes met, and this time their gazes never wavered as Judy leaned toward her until their lips joined in another kiss.

Kate felt all the months of reserve and self-discipline melting away under Judy's onslaught. She knew that one more kiss and she would give in to the wanting she had struggled to ignore for so long. Apparently, Judy knew it too, for, as she moved to kiss her yet a third time, she closed that last inch and put her arms around the woman *she* had been wanting for very nearly as long as Katherine had wanted her. They stood together in deep embrace, and Katherine's breath grew short, the burning spreading from where Judy's lips were on hers down into her belly. She pulled away, eyeing Judy with a new expression: a grudging pleasure in being won over.

"Well," she remarked huskily, "are we just going to stand here?"

"No, we're not," Judy replied evenly. With her eyes, she gave the victory back. "Lead on."

Katherine took her hand, turning out lamps as they went, and led her into the bedroom. It, too, was simple, except for the bookcase in the corner, where Katherine's gay and lesbian books reposed, along with her *Star Trek* books, a plant, a small print of Maxfield Parrish's *Ecstasy*, and a picture of Wonder Woman. Judy took them in at a glance, much more intent on the woman in front of her as she lit a candle by the bed and turned out the electric lamp.

Katherine laid back the bedcovers and then turned to Judy, slipping the pins from her shoulder-length sandy-blonde hair and shaking it out in one deft movement. Judy sighed softly through her teeth and reached to touch the thick cascade. "It's beautiful," she whispered. "You're beautiful." At last, her eyes sang, at last I can say it! And Kate heard the song, and knew her own lay within. She opened her robe, the last of her barriers, and stood before Judy, waiting for her to begin to undress. But Judy was suddenly shy again, so Kate unbuttoned the sweater and jeans and kissed her, whispering breathily, "Take them off."

She shed her robe and stood in her gown — dark blue, plain, elegant. When Judy remained in her underwear and socks, Kate chuckled softly, stepping behind her to undo the bra and help with panties and socks. Naked, Judy turned to Kate and once again embraced her. It was fire, through the silky fabric, their nipples erect and brushing. Kate momentarily stayed the renewed heat: "Judy, are you *sure?*" she whispered.

In answer, Judy knelt and began to kiss and caress her through the gown, and Kate felt her knees grow weak. She sat on the bed, stroking the auburn head and the long, strong back, as Judy began to become acquainted with Katherine's body. Kate felt the moisture between her legs soaking her gown before Judy's mouth ever found its way under the long skirt. She groaned in pleasure and lay back. Judy wrapped her arm around Katherine's hips and lifted her onto the bed, then was above her, her full breasts hanging, rubbing on Katherine's breasts, belly, and clitoris. She

14

pushed the gown up, and Katherine raised herself and slipped it off. She could feel Judy's wetness on her thighs and hips and belly. Judy was an expert lover, and she soon had Kate dangling on the edge of an orgasm. As if sensing this, she slowed her motions and pulled away a little. Katherine opened her eyes to find the gold-flecked ones smiling at her.

"Oh, Judy — if you knew how long — how many times I tried *not* to think of this!" They laughed together, and Judy slid off Kate, pulling her over her.

"Make love to me," she invoked.

As she matched Judy's skill with her fingers, tongue, lips, and body, Kate found in herself an intensity she had thought no longer possible for her. Together they climbed, reaching one peak after another, yet saving the crashing descent until the last possible moment. And it came when Judy's eager mouth found Kate's breasts as she arched backwards, her clitoris pressed against Judy's belly, her leg in Judy's crotch, her fingers milking Judy's nipple. "Oh, god!" Kate cried, finally giving herself to Judy as their orgasms seized them, carrying them on succeeding waves of pleasure until their spent bodies came to rest against one another and quiet settled over the room.

"Merry Christmas, Katherine," Judy murmured through a sleepy smile, planting a gentle goodnight kiss against her cheek.

Kate lay holding her, their bodies entwined in total repose. Well, it must be Christmas Eve by now, she thought, and a glance at the clock told her it was so. There was a stillness in her she had not known for a long time. She recognized it as the stillness of completion, and did not know how long it would last. But as she heard Judy's breathing slide into the rhythms of sleep, she thought, Yes, sleep, love — your work here tonight is done, and you deserve to rest.

15

She sighed, a soft sound in the silent room. *And my work has only begun.* Her mind drifted off to the previous late-summer day when she had seen Judy walking across campus — had picked her out of a crowd, from a block away — and felt her heart jump and her mind clamp down on it, denying herself the right to look with longing at the young woman whom she had not seen all summer. Because she had never really allowed herself to think she might become involved with Judy sexually, she had never thought ahead to this moment. Now, she knew she must consider many things, and well.

Thank god she has only one more semester of school. At least, after that, if we're still seeing each other, there won't be that pressure on our relationship.

If we're still seeing each other, she said to herself. Do I *want* to be? she asked with her customary inner honesty. Yes, came the singing reply. Oh, yes!

Judy stirred in her sleep and snuggled closer. Kate looked at her and momentarily knew how young and fresh a thing she held in her arms, nuzzling near her breast. She felt a rush of tenderness wash over her, then another question: *Am I using her youth and her wanting of me to keep me from feeling old?* She absently stroked Judy's cheek, seeing her sleeping smile at the touch. *Oh, my dear, dear Judy!* Kate bathed in the tide of feelings again and hugged her closer. She knew that, right now, she did not have the answer to her second question. She knew that she felt and believed the fifteen-year age difference was sig-nificant, and yet — *did age matter more than gender?* She pondered this, aware that she believed that gender was not the issue between lovers, but rather that they loved, truly, healthily. *Yes,* she decided, *perhaps it does matter — in a different way. People today are more accepting of same-sex relationships than they were when I was Judy's age. But that only frees people to bond without regard for gender. In this* culture, in this day and time, fifteen years, when you're on the underside of thirty, makes a big difference. There's so much growing and changing to go through during those years between twelve and thirty — I've already done all that. What if, as she grows older and changes, she discovers she doesn't want me any more? What if we didn't fit any more? What if, at thirty, she looks at a 45-year-old woman and is repulsed? Kate felt the hurt welling up within her as she contemplated loss and rejection. She knew it was one of her deepest wounds, that she had felt it at the outset of her life, that being "different" had reinforced it, that her family had tried their best to mold her over. And yet, she told herself, if this is what I really want, do I not treat myself the same way I've been treated by denying myself what there may be in this for me now?

She considered the Judy who had come to her tonight and found what she had always found: the clear, inquisitive, focused mind, seeking to apprehend the intangible, to grasp the factual, to deal honestly with herself and the world around her; a young adult with ideals which had taken some tarnishing but to which she was still committed, which she still sought to realize; the elf hiding within those mischievous eyes, with that ready laughter and mocking humor, which, mostly, she turned on herself; and, at the end of that last term, there had been something more: a deference to her, Kate, on a level that was unspoken in the student-teacher context. Could it have been the awareness, then, of what she had come to mean to Judy? Kate supposed it could have been; she knew without question now that Judy was in love with her, and she had had to acknowledge to herself tonight that there was much, much more in her than sexual desire for Judy.

She came back to the question: Could it last? And she did not know. But, she wondered, does *anyone* know? Doesn't everyone, gay or straight, take on faith that it will last, and begin their lives together in that way? Marriage is no more than a legal institution today — and there are *no* guarantees. She untangled herself and turned on her side, Judy's arm still about her. She took Judy's hand and tucked it between her breasts, backing into Judy's belly, savoring the closeness. Oh, woman, she thought, squeezing that hand, how I've loved you from afar. Can it possibly *be* what you want — what I want? Can I accept for the now, without jumping ahead into the future?

Tomorrow, she thought. Tomorrow we'll talk about this. She snuggled deeper into the embrace, then realized that she must extinguish the candle. As she leaned toward it, one of the books on the *Star Trek* shelf caught her eye and she paused. She thought of Kirk and Spock and crew, and knew that one reason she had made them all a part of her life was that they always tried — against all odds — to achieve their highest aspirations, while maintaining their deepest integrity. All right, you guys, she spoke to them mentally, I'll try too! Wonder Woman flashed a smile at her as she blew out the flame.

Tomorrow, she repeated as she sank back into Judy's sleeping embrace. Tomorrow we'll talk.

"I can't do the heels!"
Josh stands by the side of my bed, two mismatched socks in his hands, tears streaking his cheeks.
"I have such a problem with the heels!"
Six-fifty a.m. It's been a morning of problems, beginning with his waking at 5:45 and wanting breakfast. I'd muttered, "It's too early, honey," and urged him to find a little something to tide him over. A few minutes later a crash had come from downstairs, followed by Josh screaming, "Mommy, Mommy, come quick!" The dish drainer overturned, pots, pans, and silverware on the floor. Josh, in his dinosaur pajamas, stood frightened and crying in the middle of the kitchen. At 6:15, Josh had run up the stairs, a large, wet stain of carob soy milk at the center of his pajama top, a brown island for the dinosaurs to cross. "I spilled it! I spilled the chocolate milk!" (He knows it's carob, but calls it chocolate.) At 6:30, he'd appeared by the

side of my bed holding a robot, a toy computer, a Casio piano, and a tape player in his arms. "These all need batteries! And these are the only things I want to play with!"

Now he stamps his bare feet in frustration and knocks over the massage oil I'd left open on the floor by the bed. He stares at the oil oozing into the hardwood.

"Paper towels, Josh, please!"

He rushes back with one paper towel. I tend to the spill, urging him to go downstairs, finish getting dressed, and play for thirty more minutes.

"But the heels," he sniffs, as I get back into bed.

He seems three years old today instead of five, and I will not be able to get any more sleep. The source of his sudden regression lies next to me with her face against my back, her arm around my waist. Claire. It's the first time she's sleeping here on a weekend when I have Josh.

I relent and help him with his socks, then leave Claire in bed while I start getting us ready for our trip to Santa Cruz. Now that I am up, Josh ignores me. He tapes a flashlight to the ladder of his fire truck, aims it at the ceiling, and pretends that he's conducting a lecture at the planetarium. Today's topic: black holes.

When Claire comes downstairs, it begins: Why do I get to sit next to Claire at breakfast; why can't he? Why do I get to sleep in the same bed with Claire; why can't he? Why do I get to brush my teeth next to Claire; why can't he? And when we are finally loading the car with sand toys, beach towels, ice chest, he wants to know why I get to sit next to Claire in the front seat; why can't he?

I had told him there was a new special person in my life. Someone I loved very much. Did he understand? He understood. I still loved him; I could love two people. Did he know that? He knew that. Did he want to meet her? Oh yes, he wanted to meet her.

20

Now he is whining because it's taking too long; we are only in Fremont. "Why don't you try to take a nap, put your head on Snoozle?"

"I hate Snoozle. I'm not tired."

An hour later the air is sweet and my old Datsun coughs its way up the Santa Cruz Mountains. The sign reads, "Felton/Boulder Creek." "Do you remember when we were here before? And we took the train through the forest?" He doesn't answer.

It was two summers ago. I was raw, my eyes swollen from crying, my skin prickling with grief. We were to have four days alone before I would move out of the house, out of his daily life. I was leaving. I was leaving him. There was no way to separate those two facts. He slept most of the way while I obsessed about the future, the terrifying unknown. I would no longer see him every day. I'd have part-time visitation. The thought was unbearable. I woke him outside a Long's Drugs in Scotts Valley. "We're here already?" He stumbled out of the car, red blotches on his brown face, sweat glistening in his hair. "I forgot my journal. I need to buy a notebook." He understood. He loved when I wrote down the things he said. "God is round and looks like a potato. Write that down."

We stayed at a little motel in Felton, nestled in the mountains and redwoods, next to a miniature castle which we never figured out. A restaurant? Motel? On our first day we went to Roaring Camp and Big Trees Railroad, where I bought him a blue striped conductor's hat before the train ride. The train arced through the forest, steam billowing as it chugged its way up a narrow antique track, the air becoming thinner and sweeter as we ascended the jagged mountains. Josh's favorite part of the train ride was when the train had to reverse its direction because the bridge was no longer operable. Looming above us was a charred black bridge which had burned in a forest fire. Josh was mesmerized, urging me to take pictures of the burned bridge for our scrapbook.

That first night I lay awake in the king-sized motel bed listening to Josh's steady breathing as he slept next to me, his conductor's hat clutched to his chest, and I tried to trust that even with all our bridges burning behind us, we too would find alternate routes on our journey together.

Now we are finally in Santa Cruz, approaching Josh's beloved boardwalk. Josh bounces out of the car and runs ahead of us toward the arcade. His "favorite rides" are here: a small round yellow spaceship that lifts up and turns for a quarter; a small red fighter plane that shakes from side to side; an orange stagecoach that bucks back and forth. But the moment I put the quarter in the spaceship, he panics. "Don't, Mommy! Don't!" He reaches out for me to save him.

"But you loved this ride last year!"

"It's too scary! It's too scary!"

We are back on the boardwalk, passing a cotton candy stand. On our trip here that summer, I had realized that in his three years of fruit juice-sweetened cookies and granola bars, he had never had anything like cotton candy. All kids should have it at least once. "Would you like to try your first cotton candy?" I'd asked. He was beside himself with excitement, saucer eyes watching as the woman dipped the paper cone into the hot machine, turning her wrist as the pink puff grew and grew. He danced on the boardwalk with a cotton candy cone almost half his size, took his first bite, and said, "Mommy, you never told me cotton candy ee-splodes in your mouth!" Sticky red sugar clung to his lips and cheeks that entire afternoon.

But now he doesn't want any. He didn't really like it. I try to entice him to go on another favorite ride, a series of little vehicles that go round and round. All right, he sighs, as if he's being punished. He sits in a fire engine and as he passes Claire and me, he pouts because the horn doesn't work. He wants to get off. When we were here before, I used my entire "Sweetpea" ticket special on this ride, and he had tried them all — ambulance, school bus, sports car, motorcycle, over and over again.

No, he doesn't want to go in the Haunted Castle, it's too scary. No, he doesn't want to try the helicopters, they're too scary. He wants to go on the bumper cars, and cries when he measures himself against the cardboard Brutus that determines if you're tall enough to enter. He is still too small. No, he doesn't want a hot dog. No, he's not thirsty. He takes Claire's hand and walks ahead of me, leading her to the Merry-Go-Round. I trail behind them. Claire looks back to see if I'm all right. She is quiet, not used to children, afraid that she will say or do the wrong thing.

He had told me he wanted to be "girlfriends" with Claire. What does that mean? "It means she's no girlfriend of yours!" But what does it mean to be girlfriends with her? "It means we get to walk down the street together, without you."

He wants to go on the Merry-Go-Round with Claire, but not with me. Claire sits on an outside horse, catching brass rings and handing them to Josh to throw into the clown's mouth. He's delighted at first, but each time he misses the mouth his face puckers a little more until he is crying. Claire is trying to comfort him, her white-and-pink horse going up while Josh's goes down. Above me, the pastel cars of the Sky Glider coast gently across cables, and I imagine myself rising above this day, sitting high in one of the lavender coaches, staring out at the ocean.

We drive to Natural Bridges Beach, where I lay out a picnic that looks like a child's drawing: blue chips, green guacamole, orange carrot sticks, red cherry tomatoes. Josh doesn't like this; he wants what Claire is eating, a tofu salad sandwich. He wants to sit next to Claire on the blanket, he wants to put suntan lotion on Claire's back, he wants to walk to the ocean with Claire and fill his buckets up with water.

23

After lunch I lie down and close my eyes, listening to the sounds of waves and Josh building a sand structure. He is pretending he's talking into a microphone, something about mission control and rocket boosters. I drift in and out, feeling Claire's hand tracing light circles on my sun-lotioned arm. I hear numbers: ten, nine, eight ... three two one BLASTOFF! I am covered with sand, sand in my mouth, nose, eyes, ears. Josh's sand rocket has ee-sploded and landed in my face.

I taste sand in my teeth as we climb up the hill toward the splintery steps that will lead us off the beach. Why can't he sit next to Claire going home, why can't he? Because, I say. Because. Because why? Because you need a nap and you sleep better in the back. I don't need a nap! I want to sit next to Claire!

And I want to jump up and down screaming, "She's *my* girlfriend! Mine!" I can feel myself turning five, fighting with him over a precious new toy. Why do *you* get to have the new toy? Because I'm the grown-up, that's why.

We drive through the forest in silence. I am wondering if Claire will ever spend time with us again. I am wondering if she is wondering whether she can have a lover with a child. I am wondering if she can ever find me sexy again. I am a mean mommy with a sunburn and sticky hands and guacamole fingerprints on my shorts and sand in my eyelashes.

I am burning with frustration, anger, hot red shoulders. But now that Josh and I are the same age, it's easier to understand what he's feeling. I think about his confusion, the way he's been trying to fit the pieces together like parts of the Lego cities he builds in the early-morning hours. I see Josh staring at me over a bean taco and announcing, "First I came out of Mama Louise's tummy and then I came out of your tummy." Josh standing at the toilet singing an impromptu song: "Where is my daddy, why don't I have a daddy?" Josh in the backseat as we drive up Fruitvale

Avenue: "Mama , Louise lets me eat McDonald's and you don't. That's why you separated." Josh as he spins a dreidel and peels the gold foil off a carob coin: "The Christians fight the Jews. I know, because Mama Louise fights you."

And now Josh is asleep in the backseat, Snoozle, his pink-and-purple pillow creature, wedged under his chin, sand sparkling like powdered sugar on his dark arms, exhausted from a day of trying to fit yet another Lego piece into the city.

That evening, when he is bathed and dressed in his outer-space pajamas that came with a small space shuttle which he lost immediately but asks for every time, I tell him we need to have a little talk before we read a story. He lowers his eyes. "Little talks" usually mean bad news, or he's done something wrong. I reassure him that there's nothing to worry about. If only I could pull out a bedtime story about a nonbiological mother who has a new girlfriend. None of the books will do. Claire is not a stepparent, I am not a daddy, Josh is not white. We are nowhere, just as we were nowhere during the breakup, and no books were even close except one about two dinosaurs getting divorced. But even there, one dinosaur wore a suit and tie, the other an apron and high heels. It is up to me to create the bridges that fill in the gaps.

When Josh was four, I sat him down before the Lesbian and Gay Freedom Day parade with a yellow pad and pen and drew pictures of two women, two men, and a man and a woman. The two women love each other and they're lesbians, I told him. The two men love each other and they're gay men. The man and the woman love each other and they're heterosexuals, or you can call them straight people. "Let's go with straight," he said. I explained that I was a lesbian and that there were bad people who didn't think lesbians and gay men should have rights, and that's why we were marching. We were proud, and we deserved to have rights. Moments later, Josh ran in circles around the kitchen yelling, "Hi, Lesbian! Hi, Mommy Lesbian!" The back door was open and his words resonated out the screen door, over rooftops. I felt myself tightening. But how could I tell him to lower his voice when we were in the middle of a discussion on gay pride?

Now it is time to be creative again. I take out the deck of cards that came with his toy computer, his "disks." I show him a card with a little girl doing a puzzle and say, "This is me spending time alone." A card with a pink hippo and a purple mouse on its back becomes Mommy and Josh spending time together. A little boy at the beach, putting starfish and shells into a box, becomes Josh spending time alone. A giraffe talking to a monkey becomes Mommy and Claire spending time together. A smiling sun, moon, and star become Mommy and Josh and Claire spending time together. Two children fishing — one catching a tin can, the other a boot — become Claire spending time with Josh. I explain each card: Sometimes I just want to be with you, sometimes I need time alone, sometimes I want to be with Claire ... But if you act whiny and difficult, Claire won't want to spend time with you and we can never have this card — the sun, moon, and star — or this card — the two children fishing.

He touches each card gently, and tells me he understands. I am five years old again but this time I am feeling his feelings, not mine. I want to take his pain away. Two mommies who don't live together any more. No daddy. And now this new person who steals me away from him. It can be so hard sometimes to do the heels.

When Josh was two, we spent a weekend in Tahoe with some friends and their baby. After putting the children to sleep we started playing pinochle. A short while later, we smelled something burning in the cabin. We found Josh, sitting up in bed, hypnotized by a lamp burning a hole into

26

his mattress, curls of smoke rising toward his face. He knew he shouldn't have taken the lamp off the wall, so he was afraid to call out for help. I worry now about the sadness burning inside him, his inability to cry for help directly. I put my arm around him and read him *The Good Wood Bear,* about a goose and a bear building a birdhouse together, carving the door into the shape of a heart.

It's 6:00 a.m., another Sunday morning. On Josh's train place mat on the kitchen table sits a bowl of Fruitio's — new-age Fruit Loops — a box of vanilla soy milk, a spoon. Josh's clothes are laid out on the living room couch. A tape of *Wind in the Willows* sits in the VCR. I hear him in the bathroom singing "Beat It." I leave the warmth of blue flannel sheets and Claire's body and meet him in the hallway.

"Hi, sweetie."

"Mom, come look what I've done!" He takes my hand and leads me downstairs. "See, they're all wearing clothes!" His "dollies" are sitting on the couch in a row: Lion is wearing Josh's witch costume and Halloween cape; Snow-bear is wearing a crown, a necklace, and a Chinese vest; Alfred is in a gold lamé scarf with a yarmulke on his head.

"They're wonderful!" I say. "All dressed up for a party!"

"Not a party," he corrects me. "An important meeting."

I show him his breakfast and clothes, then put on the VCR. We cuddle together with the dollies for the beginning of *Wind in the Willows,* Judy Collins mournfully singing the theme song. "I'd like to go back to bed for another hour. Is that okay?"

"Sure," he says, "you guys have fun."

"I love you."

"I love you too," he says, "for a hundred years."

When Claire and I come down, Josh is dressed, his breakfast is eaten, his dishes are in the sink, and he is now watching a tape of *The Dark Crystal.* The dollies have all changed outfits: Lion is now the Empress, Snowbear the Witch, Alfred the Queen. Josh runs up to Claire and hugs her around the waist, then asks if he can go with her to get the Sunday paper.

I grind coffee beans while they're gone, scramble eggs, chop red bell peppers. I feel like Dustin Hoffman at the end of *Kramer vs. Kramer,* when he and his son can finally make breakfast in harmony, the earlier chaos transformed into a choreographed ritual. The cat cries at the front door. When I open the door and look up the street, I see Josh and Claire returning. They are holding hands, each carrying a piece of the Sunday paper. Josh is beaming. His wish has come true, at least for this morning: He and Claire are girlfriends, walking down the street without me.

ONE SUNDAY MORNING

SHELLEY ANDERSON

Summers were always difficult, and this one was more difficult than most. Mother had found a job sewing in the factory for the summer, because Daddy's business wasn't too good lately, and now Sarah had to drag her little sister with her everywhere.

When school had ended, the summer months had spread before Sarah like one of those prairies in the books, endless and free. Joannie was going to take the swimming lessons for kids at the new pool, and Sarah would be free to read and bicycle around to her heart's content. But the pool had been closed abruptly, on account of those strangers from up north, and the prairie shrank as Sarah was restricted to endless baby-sitting.

"Communists, just Godless Communists," hissed the neighbor lady, her mouth full of clothespins. She gave the sheet a vicious snap and then stabbed it on the line. "Outside agitators — you girls stay away from them," Mr. Jamison warned, handing Sarah the orange popsicles from behind his counter. "They just want the same things for their children we want for ours, but this is the wrong way to go about it," Sarah's mother explained. Sarah's father said nothing, but the whole family knew his silence was as powerful as all of their words put together.

A few days before that Sunday morning, Sarah had run to the side of their white frame house to get away from Joannie's endless questions and chatter. The trees and bushes surrounding the house made it seem like a forest, Sarah's own private sanctuary. It wasn't fair that she had to spend her whole vacation watching over a baby. She had had plans of her own for this summer, adventures like exploring the abandoned ice factory just outside of town or trying to catch a glimpse of the big 'gator that was supposed to live in Jackson's Lake. Feeling much put upon, Sarah threw herself to the ground. The shade and the cool earth were as soothing as the litany of wrongs she kept reciting to herself.

Sarah had almost lulled herself to sleep when Joannie's voice broke in. Furious, Sarah swung around and knocked the small offering of daisies and black-eyed Susans out of her sister's hand. For an instant, Joannie's face was blank with shock. Then her loving smile crumbled and she began to cry.

The rejection also crushed Sarah. Watching her sister's face change was like watching clouds obscure the sun — the accustomed warmth disappeared and something hidden suddenly sprang out, cold and frightening. Hurting, she realized then, had consequences, both for the one who endured and the one who inflicted the pain.

Sarah ran, right into the arms of her father, who had seen everything. She would have welcomed a reprimand, even a slap, for making her sister cry. Instead, he said nothing, just rocked her as she sobbed in his arms. His silence was as deep as understanding, and as forgiving. Only later, when Joannie was enfolded also, did he whisper to them, "You got to love each other."

That Sunday began with the usual smells of ham sizzling in the frying pan and coffee boiling. Sarah and Joannie fought for the place of honor — beside their father on the walk to church, holding his calloused hand that could fix a bicycle and flip an omelette with equal grace. Their mother, with a grin, settled the argument by walking behind.

The sun beat down, bullying the okra and tomato plants, and heat waves danced off the asphalt. The family walked past the courthouse, under the shadow of the granite Confederate soldier, who eternally shoved powder down the muzzle of a stone gun. Sarah suppressed an urge to tuck his gray bedroll under his arm, because it always looked about to roll off the pedestal. The soldier stared with blind eyes at the red brick courthouse. Inside, during the week, one of Sarah's cousins recorded the town's births, deaths, and marriages. Unlike during the week, no old black men waited this morning on the steps for farmers to hire them to pick oranges or chop firewood.

The bells were ringing as they entered and found their seats. Mother had already handed Joannie some scrap paper and a crayon, knowing the child would soon be squirming. The preaching was boring but Sarah loved church anyway. The psalms and the singing were beautiful. Watching the dust motes dancing on the shafts of sunlight from the tall windows and the smiles of the congregation made her feel happy, as if she belonged to these people and would be cared for by them. The happiness made her want to be good. She experienced a yearning she could not explain when the preacher talked about the necessity of loving kindness.

They always sat near the back. Once, wanting to see the baptisms better, Sarah had asked if they could sit up

31

front. "The closer the pew, the farther from God," their father had answered with a wink. Sarah suspected it had more to do with the fact that those up front wore fancier clothes. Judy Warren, who was in Sarah's same fifth-grade class, wore white gloves in the summer and a coat with a fur collar in the winter, and always sat in the second pew.

It didn't bother Sarah too much, as in the back she had the special window — the one with Mary in it holding the dimpled baby Jesus. Sarah had had enough of babies this summer, but she loved the rich blue color of Mary's robe and the tender look in the dark brown eyes. It'd be fun to live in a barn, she thought. Mama always says I act like I'm living in one anyway.

The window's colors were beautiful with the sun streaming through. Sometimes the black shadow of a bird would sweep across the window, unexpected and surprising.

A passing cloud suddenly blocked out the sun, dimming the colors as Sarah watched in fascination — then just as suddenly disappeared, so the blues and reds and browns leapt to life again, like flames in a fire. Light and shadow continued to play hide-and-seek throughout the service. The girl only half listened to the preacher exhorting the congregation. "Call them freedom riders or call them troublemakers, but let us keep from violence," he said. "We are all God's children, white or black. We all have our designated places. We are commanded to love those who persecute us."

After church another satisfying ritual began. The family walked in comfortable silence down Main Street to the Red Wagon Cafeteria. Joannie, happy to be released once more into motion and air, ran ahead. She spotted the signs on the bus station's restroom doors.

"Sarie, I know my letters! M-E-N — what's that spell?" she asked. Her father answered. "Oh. L-A-D-I-E-S — that's girls," she said, guessing proudly. She turned to the third door. The sign had been removed recently, but the faded outline of the letters stood out against the darker wood, like a newly healed scar against older skin.

"C-O-L-O-R-E-D. What's that spell, Sarie?"

But Sarah ignored her. She was already dreaming of lunch, of the chicken and dumplings floating in the savory broth, buttery corn sticks, and the blueberry pie. She would slide the heavy tray across the shiny bars to the cashier, where a black man in a short white jacket would then smile at her and carry the tray to the table. They would sit at a round table and enjoy the luxury of an air conditioner. Her father would have thin slices of roast beef in thick gravy and let her take sips from his coffee cup.

Not until she bumped into her mother did she realize something was wrong. Her mother grabbed Sarah's arm, preventing her from going any further. Craning her neck, Sarah could see the crowd gathering around the cafeteria. Then she saw the demonstrators.

There were only six of them, carrying signs that had been neatly hand-lettered. A young man, his skin the color of milky coffee, led the group in song. The one white man in the circle, an older man in a plaid coat, kept his eyes strictly in front of him. They held their signs and circled in front of the cafeteria's entrance, seemingly oblivious to the jeers and catcalls. Sarah had the strange realization that the older white man was not the one in charge of the group.

She looked at the faces in the crowd around her. They were ugly and spitting out even uglier words. The rising, choking anger in the air frightened her and made her want to run. Someone was going to get hurt, and she didn't want to see it. It wasn't fair to shout at people, especially as there were at least three times as many people in the crowd as in the circle.

Looking back at the circle, Sarah noticed the black girl for the first time. She was walking alongside a plump older woman who held a paper fan with a picture of Jesus on it. The girl's hair was neatly braided, and she wore the same kind of blue skirt that Sarah wore to school. Her white blouse made her skin look darker, richer. She was, Sarah realized with a shock, only a few years older than Joannie, almost Sarah's age. There was a look of quiet determination on her face. On her sign were the words "Love Your Neighbor As Yourself."

It's not fair, Sarah sang to herself. They're only doing what's right. Let's go home, she tried to shout, but the words stuck in her throat. There were faces in the crowd she knew she should recognize, but hate had twisted their features so she could not tell who they were. The white faces began to blur and run into each other, and the jeers grew louder. The black girl gripped her sign and kept singing.

Someone jostled Sarah's arm. Frightened, she glanced to her side and saw her father pushing his way through the crowd. Relief flooded Sarah. He would protect the black girl, just as he would have protected Sarah if she had been in the circle. Her father respected bravery. Anybody who could remain so calm, faced with such anger and shouting, was brave. He knew about how to love and what was fair. Once he rescues her we can all go home, Sarah thought.

Her father was almost next to the singing girl. Sarah was proud of him and afraid for him, afraid of what the crowd might do to him when he helped the girl. Then she watched as her father looked into the girl's eyes and spit in her face.

Years later, she would puzzle over and over again as to how this had changed her, this first realization that her father could be wrong. She knew it had led to her first separation, her first sense of self as someone different from her parents.

Even later, ashamed, she wondered how it had changed the black girl's life. That Sunday morning, however, she could only take her father's hand automatically and stumble after him, to a home that felt no longer safe. She did know then that it would be the last time she'd ever hold her father's hand.

SMOKE SIGNALS

JAYNE RELAFORD BROWN

G ramps has finally found the cigarettes. We're taking a load of new old tools and magazines he bought at yard sales over to the side of the house when he sees the pack where I've left it under my tree.

"These yours, T.J.?" he asks me, kicking the pack with his toes, getting dirt all over it on purpose.

"Yeah," I say, real casual, as if it's nothing. As if I've been smoking for years, even though I'm only thirteen. "Yeah. What about it?"

"Well, T.J.," he says, slow, then takes off his hat and rubs his forehead like he's getting a splitting headache. "Well, it's just not like you, T.J. You haven't caused us any problems to speak of since you came. If your mama's going to get herself out of that psychiatrist hospital, she doesn't need to be worrying about what you're up to." He plants the shovel he's carrying into the ground and shakes out his ratty old handkerchief.

"T.J.?" he says. "What do you say we just not tell your Grander? No sense making her upset." Gramps mops off his freckled, sunburned head. "You knock it off, kiddo, and we just won't mention it again. Case closed." He fakes a smile and sticks out his hand, palm up, for our old secret handshake. Then he rubs at his head again and kind of sighs, and tells me why don't I go unload these magazines before dark. And that's the extent of it.

✳

Sundays they always drive up to visit my mom. And since I'm so responsible, so they say, I get to hang around the house by myself all day. Loads of fun, because the closest kid my age lives about two miles away. I try asking again when I'll get to go up with them and see Mom, but Grander kind of tears up and says, "Well, honey, she's getting stronger. We'll see." Getting stronger. As if I'm gonna want her to carry me or something.

Grander tells me she thinks Mom's embarrassed for me to see her all depressed. I don't care. I'd just like to see her and maybe we could talk a little. She used to get a real kick out of hearing what went on at school. Even after she got so bad that she wouldn't go out of the house, I could still almost always make her laugh by telling her stories. And believe me, I've been doing nothing but saving up stories for months, since nobody around here seems to think the same things are funny that we do. When they ask you about school around here, it's like when some people say "How are you?" and you know the only answer they want to hear is "Fine." So, fine. Fine. I want to tell them I could handle seeing Mom, and maybe I could even make her feel better, probably even better than they could, but Grander's still looking pretty weepy, so I don't press it.

Gramps tells me he'll give me a couple of bucks if I look around the yard while they're gone and stack all the loose wood against the garage. Maybe we'll even go down to the beach and make a big bonfire with it one of these days, he says. Uh-huh. I've heard those kind of promises before. First my mom kept telling me she was going to take me up to see snow last winter. Then, when she had to go in the hospital, Gramps promised me he'd take me. But here it is the middle of summer and who knows if I'll ever see snow.

Grander's waving at me with her soggy hanky as they drive off, so I wave back till they're out of sight and start hunting around for wood. Any time you do a job around this house, it seems as if you'll never finish. Every time I turn around, more junk appears. The backyard looks like a bombed house with just the furniture left standing. Gramps set an old wooden hat rack next to some rusted wrought-iron furniture — a love seat and chairs with an end table that he bought last year at a yard sale. Piled next to it is a pickup truck's worth of bricks that Gramps and I carted from a torn-down building five years ago. We stacked them by what used to be my swing set, which made it a good place to catch lizards, but then black widows moved in, too.

Gramps is always finding great deals on stuff he thinks he might eventually need, but it's like this wood I'm stacking for this supposed bonfire someday — it'll just sit out here and rot. His whole patio is heaped up to my waist with boxes of magazines Gramps says he might want to read one of these days. Mom told me once it would be a blessing if the whole place burned down, as long as nobody got hurt.

Seems as if I gather wood for hours, and I haven't even covered half the yard. Even kicking crates and boards apart is getting pretty boring, and the folks probably won't be home till after dark. Grander told me she left a TV dinner in the freezer, but I swear if I eat any more of that rubber chicken and plastic potatoes, I'll puke.

I look around again at this pile of lumber I've dragged up here, then back at the tons more of it still all over the yard. Mom told me once she offered to rent Gramps a dumpster for his birthday and help him haul it all away, but he didn't think that was too funny. I stack all the wood I've collected and go to get some more, but my heart just isn't in it any more. Then I remember the same kid that bought the cigarettes for me gave me a lighter, too. I lean one of the crate slats up against the step by the back door of the garage, and start kicking it into smaller pieces.

✳

By the time the grandparents get back, I've pretty much forgotten about my personal bonfire, until Gramps pulls me aside when Grander goes to the store.

"Look, T.J.," he says, trying to rub out one of those headaches again. "That little stunt you pulled out back could have been pretty dangerous. What if that whole pile had caught and set off the garage?"

I start to square off with him, but all I can think of is how many headaches he keeps getting and how I could hear sort of crying sounds from their room last night. So I apologize instead.

"I'm sorry, Gramps," I tell him. "I just thought it would be fun to roast some marshmallows, was all. Like the bonfire on the beach we were going to have. I guess that was pretty stupid."

Gramps looks off. "Don't worry about it, kiddo," he says after a little bit. "I cleaned the ashes up so your Grander wouldn't see them and get upset. She's got a lot to worry about right now, with your mother and all." He pats his dry old hand on my shoulder. "So let's keep mum on this one," he says, still patting me with that stiff hand. "We'll get out to the beach one of these days and roast marshmallows there, like I said. Hey," he says, looking surprised, "I still owe you a trip to the snow."

＊

I've taken to borrowing Grander's magnifying glass when I get bored. It's neat how the sun will build up enough heat through the lens to burn just about anything. I used to do mostly snails and ants, or those plastic dinosaurs and Indians, but lately I've been using paper, and getting to where I can write pretty well by aiming the light ray to burn through, and moving the glass just in time.

That's what I'm doing when Grander comes out in the backyard to hang clothes.

"So, T.J., how's school?" she asks me around a clothespin clamped between her teeth.

"Fine," I tell her.

I sit there burning paper the whole time she hangs two baskets of clothes. When she's not looking at me, I watch her. If you look at her quick, she looks a lot like my mom. Same soft curly hair, but just more gray. Same laugh lines around her eyes, but lots deeper.

When she's finished, she walks by me with her baskets and looks down at what I'm doing. I think I'm about to catch it for the magnifying glass. So I just keep burning, and see what she's going to say.

"Well, T.J.," she says, "this is nicer than burning up your toys or little bugs." She picks up the paper, holds it to the light, and examines the crispy black H-E-L-P I've burnt into it.

"That's very good, honey," she says. "My handwriting was never that good at your age, even with a pencil."

She goes up the steps swinging her laundry baskets and laughing like she's made up a joke. I haven't heard her laugh in a long time, so I smile for her when she looks back and says, "Have fun, dear."

Next weekend before they go visit Mom, Gramps gives me the money I earned from hauling wood. "Have a good time," they say, and off they go like always. Since there's nothing better to do, I decide to walk to the store. I play a couple of video games and buy some candy and a box of Diamond matches. A thousand of them.

When I get back, I stick a TV dinner in the oven and go out to the garage. That place is worse than the yard, full of new junk Gramps buys at yard sales and old junk he says he doesn't have the heart to part with. It's packed to the rafters with mattresses, broken bicycles, even my old baby crib, and one corner's all piled up with my mom's and my things from the apartment we used to have. I see a bare spot on the floor by our stuff. I scoot sideways through a nearly clear pathway, clear the dust off a little square area, and lean up against Mom's old throw rug. After a while, I start lighting those thousand matches, one at a time, and stack them up, log-cabin style, on the floor. I let each match burn down as long as I can stand it before I blow it out, and then set it on top of the stack. Seems like I get better at holding each match longer, because after a while it doesn't hurt as much. The whole deal takes so long that my TV dinner gets burnt to a crisp.

✺

Grander and Gramps look worse than usual when they get home. I ask them what's the matter, but Gramps says something about my mom just having a bad day. He tells me not to worry, though, because they're going to try a new medicine for her, and then something called ECT shock something, if that doesn't work.

Grander smells the burnt smell right away and when she sees the black chicken lying there in the trash, she picks it up and starts crying like crazy all of a sudden about "ruined, ruined." Gramps puts his arms around her and takes her off to their bedroom. He tells me not to stay up too late.

41

After I'm pretty sure they're asleep, I sneak out to the garage and stuff the stack of matches into a plastic bag, and rub the cement with a corner of our old rug until the ashes don't show.

✳

All week, I hear Grander and Gramps arguing about whether it does any good to go up and see her any more, that maybe they just make her more upset. But every time I show up in the room, they stop talking or say shouldn't I be out playing in the sunshine. It's pretty clear they don't want to talk to me about her, or anything.

They finally decide to stay home this weekend, and tell me they think Mom should have a little rest from their visits. Just to let him know I'm interested, I ask Gramps how about that trip to the beach, since he hasn't had a weekend free in a long time, and I know there's no snow now. Well, he says, as usual, and pats me on the shoulder, then sighs and rubs his head as usual. Well, T.J., he says, of course he'd love to, but he needs to kind of be around for Grander right now, and all. So why don't I just plan on playing or whatever I usually do when they're gone.

The pack of cigarettes is still under the tree. It's been pretty dry this summer, so they're okay, but dirt gets in my mouth when I try to smoke them. I take them back into the garage to my little cement spot, then I lean up against our old rug and light up.

I sit out there a pretty long time, and after a while I start wondering how long it would be before they'd notice I was gone, and wonder if I was kidnapped or dead or something. It's getting pretty cold, so I unroll our rug and wrap it around me, Indian style, to wait. It's funny how that rug still smells like our old place after all this time.

I sit smoking another cigarette and wrapped up in this old rug that smells like home. I don't know if my mom will get better so we can have our own house again, or even come back here so we can tell each other stories. I start feeling mad at her for going away, but then right off I get scared, because I don't want to think about her never coming back. I remember all the times I really must have worn her out, when she was trying her best to take care of me, being alone and all. Then I feel pretty lousy.

After a while I get pissed off at Grander and Gramps. How long is it going to take before they notice I'm gone? I'm sick of telling them everything's fine and hearing promises about bonfires and snow. But right on top of that I hear a voice like my mom's ask how can I be mad at them because they're doing their best, and taking care of me. I think about those headaches of Gramps's, and Grander crying all the time, and how they look really, really old when they fall asleep in their recliner chairs and their faces sag, and I start feeling scared again. Mad, sad, and scared all comes together at once, hot, like that sun through the magnifying glass until I feel like I'm going to burn up.

And the next thing I know, I've got that cigarette up at my arm and I put it to my skin for a minute just to see if I can take it. And when I take the cigarette away, there's this really perfect little round burn. So I set another one right up next to it, and a couple more after that. I find out I can take it longer each time, so I go to work on another row right below.

The weird thing is, I feel better. The burns kind of take the edge off things. I wrap our old rug tighter around me, snuggle into it until I really get the smell of being home. After a while, I light another cigarette. The light outside fades out until all I can see is its orange tip glowing and changing — black, gray, orange — as it burns the paper on its way toward my fingers, and every once in a while, I can feel ash fall against the skin of my arms, as soft as snow must be.

BUZZARD TAKES FLIGHT

IVY BURROWES

"**A** *real* friend is someone you can be naked around
without necessarily resorting to sex," Buzzard told
me once, plumped on her brocade sofa in the raw. Her
breasts dragged heavily against her as she moved, spooning
Sara Lee straight from the carton.

"I'll drink to that," I winked and looked quickly away,
contemplating the effervescence of burgundy in the warm
circle of her fire and feeling conspicuously dressed. In those
days I'd drink to anything ... The comfortable silence
stretched like an enduring filament between us, the flickering blaze warming my toes, as well as the crystalline
skeleto.1 of frost that adorned the outer pane of her big
picture window. She hadn't bothered to draw the drapes so
I stared out, fascinated by the blush of moonshine on the
snow, sparkling through an oriel of winter's icy marrow.

"No, really," Buzzard insisted. "People invest a fortune,
not to mention their time and energy, buying jewelry,

clothing, cosmetics, cars even, just to disguise their nudity. We're ashamed of our flesh, when the flesh, after all, is the fundamental thing — the only thing we have in common. It's where we live." She cast Sara aside with a fervor. "It's true, think about it. Without bodies we are nothing."

"Agreed," I smiled, snuggling down into the barrier of my bulky sweater in anticipation of a knock at the door. "Your paperboy's on his way up the walk. Care to acquaint him with your theory?"

"Holy shit!" Buzzard flapped from the room, a discombobulated formation of feet and elbows, tits and ass, her long brown hair like feathers flying.

"I was getting chilly anyway," Buzzard said, returning presently, bundled up in baggy sweats and a t-shirt that read, "Wear Life Like a Loose Garment."

"You owe me for the paper," I offered smugly, and we both laughed.

✳

Margaret is the name they gave her. Peggy would've suited, or Maggie, or Meg, but she preferred Buzzard. Whenever anyone asked, as they invariably did, how she acquired such a brutal name, she would reply with an offhand smile, "I just picked it up, I guess."

Actually, she picked it out. When her family moved up north from Arkansas she introduced herself to everyone in town as Buzzard, extending a pudgy hand, and that was that. Down south, she confessed to me years later, she'd been Peggy Sue.

"So? What's wrong with that?" I asked, all wide-eyed Yankee innocence.

"Have you ever heard a southern pig farmer rounding up the herd?" she demanded ungraciously. "'Souee pig, piggy souee' ... I felt like a chunk of livestock or something, in pigtails and chubbette clothes. My formative years were miserable, believe me!"

"But why *Buzzard?*"

"Oh, I don't know. It sounds sort of earthy, don't you think? Predatory without being ostentatious."

"I suppose," I shrugged.

"Look, I was an ugly fat kid with a southern drawl and rich parents, to boot. I had to do something."

"You're not ugly, and you're not fat." I was always telling her that, infusing her with self-esteem.

"You're right. I'm not ugly, but I'll always be fat," she said.

✳

Throughout high school, perpetually preoccupied with her weight, Buzzard dieted incessantly and critiqued each day, good or bad, in terms of calories consumed.

"Are you having a good time, Buzzard?" someone might ask at a party.

"A hundred 'n' fifty calories in this tiny can of beer, and I had a burger for lunch," she'd respond, frowning.

Buzzard calculated her life not in birthdays and Christmases past but with intricate formulas delineating gross tonnage gained and lost. On New Year's Eve, 1969, she announced at midnight that she'd shed two average-sized people in a single decade. "Of course, I gained three," she chortled, raising her glass. "Bring on the seventies."

Our first year of college found me waiting tables for tuition and struggling for intellectual mediocrity, while she made A's effortlessly. When I complained, she said by way of consolation, "At least you're not fat," as though that justified everything. Some great equalizer.

The following year Buzzard was adopted into a feminist group comprised, in part, by a circus of vocally militant lesbians who finally impressed upon her, through means that had certainly never occurred to me, that there was just more of her to love. And that they did, much to my consternation.

After college, Buzzard went to Europe for a year before assuming her obligatory position in the family business, and I went on to work my way through graduate school. She dropped me a line now and then, posted from Rome or Paris or Athens, and I despised her for leading a life that I longed for and couldn't afford, but then I moved to California, got a tan, satisfied my latent curiosity with a beautiful woman named Lisa (an affair which, sadly, didn't even outlast the tan), and I didn't have the energy to resent Buzzard any more. When her father died, I was there. She flew out to the coast whenever she could. We vowed never to slip so far apart that we couldn't catch up over lunch, although I never did tell her about Lisa. I thought then that when the time was right, eventually, I would.

When my mother died I sold my condo, bought a secondhand jeep, and went home. L.A. wasn't the mecca of civilization for me any longer, and I couldn't tolerate the glitzy, gun-shy atmosphere that polluted the city, nor did I want my first book to be born there.

Buzzard was waiting in the aisles for me as I surrendered myself to the old hometown. I was totally happy with the prospect of seeing her, finally free to *be* with her, until I discovered that, in my absence, Buzzard had taken a beau.

"So what's his name?" I asked, treading water to keep from sinking.

"Norm. Norm Schneider." Buzzard tossed her long auburn hair defiantly. "No cracks."

"Whatever do you mean? It sounds like a nice, *normal* name to me," I sighed. "What's he like?"

"Well, he *is* nice, intelligent, handsome, and he doesn't mind that I'm fat."

"You're not fat."

47

"I know, but most men perceive me as fat. Women are more tolerant, but men don't differentiate between fatty tissue and bone structure, let's face it."

"Buzzard, you're crazy."

"I'm not. What the hell do you know about it, anyway? You eat like a pig and swill enough liquor to bloat the entire state of Kansas, and you never gain an ounce. I hate you for that."

"Yeah, I'm really in great shape," I agreed and emptied my glass. "A hack writer, perpetually broke, probably an alcoholic."

"Probably. But you know what I mean. Actually, I *do* prefer women," she said, "and I'm more comfortable eating with women as a rule. I'd make a dandy lesbian, if I could only get past the introductions. It's awkward as hell waltzing into a corporate party or a stockholder's meeting with a big dyke on your arm. I mean, with most people, even you, damn it, all one has to say is 'I'm a homo...' and they freak out. It doesn't matter if you go on to say that you're a homeowner, or a Homo sapiens, or a homophobic buffoon. No one's listening any more. People don't take lesbians seriously."

It didn't seem like an opportune time to tell her I'd become one. I chewed off my longest fingernail. "Norman they take seriously?" I queried to distract her.

"Sure, he's bigger than I am, and he has a beard."

"Oh, well then. As long as you're not going to pretend that it's *love* or anything..."

She glared at me defiantly then burst out laughing. "Damn your ass."

Only the thing with Norman didn't last very long.

"What, exactly, happened?" I insisted, silently determining that Norman's abrupt evacuation might be just the thing to return Buzzard to her senses. She was sniffling over the phone.

"He met someone, at that stupid party I obliged him to attend last weekend. An inconsequential little tart. Leslie." She spat the name. "She's about five-eight, a hundred pounds, max, with a matching IQ, color-coordinated, blonde. A nothing little bitch. She works for me, for Chris'sake."

"Are you going to fire her?"

"Hell, no. Firing's too good for her. I'm going to infest her boudoir with filarial worms and—"

"What?" I choked. "Filarial worms?"

"Insidious carriers of elephantiasis, and I hope they both swell up like—"

"Do you want me to come over?"

"Will you? And bring something to eat?" she brightened.

"Okay. What?"

"A cheesecake," she decided immediately. "Norman detests cheesecake."

※

For several weeks Buzzard was more depressed than I'd ever seen her, in bitter contrast to her typically ruthless good cheer, and she lost weight, although even she admitted that she'd probably recover and that Norman was a total loss in bed anyway.

When her smile returned, it was more fragile than before, a gauzy facade too transparent to disguise the agony festering behind her eyes. She refused to discuss Norman, which was fine, but she was cranky and disagreeable about everything, as though she expected, by her demeanor, to keep the world a safe distance away, and me as well.

When Buzzard announced her intention to go abroad, I was actually relieved. Her sullen expression had become my burden, intensifying the confusing realization that I had tarried too long on the precipice of actually falling in love with her, my dearest, most trusted, and suddenly straight, it seemed, lifelong friend. I couldn't reconcile myself to the taste of bile, the bitter irony.

I really began to pine for her, though, after she'd been gone for months and months without a word, and especially after I finished the book and celebrated all alone.

Buzzard dropped by to see me when she got back. She just showed up at the door as though she'd been out to get cigarettes, instead of incommunicado for nearly a year. I answered the bell with the newly arrived galley copy of my novel in hand.

"Buzzard!" I squealed, hugging her soundly. "I'm so glad you're back. Look!" I jabbed the manuscript up under her nose, realizing only then that she didn't look like a woman replenished by an extended vacation. She looked like hell, as a matter of fact.

"Buzzard, what's wrong?" I retreated from her, scowling. "You look so..."

"I know. Beautiful, huh?"

"You're so thin," I smiled weakly. Her broad shoulders sagged, sporting an uncharacteristically stylish outfit that she wore with all the grace of a flimsy wire coat hanger.

"Your majesty," I curtsied, and issued her in.

"I stumbled upon this great diet," she said hesitantly. "Worked pretty well, don't you think?" She turned so I could see her, all of her, or what little was left, holding her jacket open without disturbing the turban wrapped severely about her head.

"I'm not sure, Buzz," I admitted. "You look very 'sheik,' indeed, but why so pale? Have you been to some sort of spa or something?"

"Um ... sort of," she said absently, fondling the book. "So this is it. Can I read it, finally?"

"Sure," I smiled, swaggering, "although I imagine it'll be much more impressive in hardback."

"Humph," she snorted. "I can't wait."

"Can I fix you a drink?" I inquired. "I truly feel the need of one."

"Thanks, no. This diet," she squirmed.

"No alcohol? How pagan."

"Do you have any ginger ale?"

"Nope. How about coffee?"

She trailed me into the kitchen. "Unh-uh. Milk?"

"Come on, Buzzard. What kind of diet is this?" I demanded. "Milk? Yuck. You never drink milk."

"I do now," she assured me.

I mixed myself a gin and tonic and, grimacing, gave her the milk. She sat down at the table and flipped through the book idly.

"Where the hell have you been, anyway? What's your secret?" I persisted. "Not one of those radical weight-loss programs, I hope."

"Ha! Radical weight loss," she laughed. "That's it. Pretty radical, I'd say." Then her amusement dissipated and a grim shadow darkened her face. "Sit down, kid," she said.

I regarded her suspiciously.

"I had a baby," Buzzard pronounced carefully. "It's Norman's, of course, although he knows nothing about it, and never will, I hope."

"Oh, right," I smirked, gulping my drink. "Where are you keeping this child, in your purse?"

"She's in Germany, with her nanny, believe it or not. I know it sounds crazy, but there you are. I'm going back next week. I only came home to clean up the residue of my life here. I sold the business," she finished flatly, nursing her milk.

It was my turn to pale. "You're kidding," I insisted. I thought I knew everything about her and suddenly she was a total stranger. "Most women gain weight with a baby, Buzzard, they don't shrink. What's this all about?"

"I just told you," Buzzard chuckled. "I knew you'd have trouble with this. Her name is Anna," she said, rifling through her bag. "Here's a picture." She produced a photograph of a remarkably healthy infant against a field of blue. "She doesn't look a thing like Norman, I'm afraid. She takes after me, poor thing, but she is cute, isn't she?"

"Yeah, cute," I agreed miserably, handing the snapshot back. "Buzzard, you amaze me." I finished my drink. "A baby?"

"Well, mix yourself another and take a deep breath," she warned. "There's more."

I did as she advised. I mixed that drink, but I never did finish it.

✳

Anna looks quite like her mother, even still — big bones, a ready smile, apt, capable hands, and thick dark hair flowing untrained. She has her mother's sense of humor, too. She plays the piano. And she's bright. Oh boy, is she bright.

Anna calls me Mama, a form of address that I never in a million years expected to answer to, but wouldn't exchange for anything. Well, maybe one thing, but what's done is done.

Buzzard died a few months after Anna was born, but the tumor that killed her was present even before Anna's birth. They grew simultaneously, flourishing inside of Buzzard, who had never been able to grow anything. The fertile cancer prospered, like tomatoes in a hothouse, and eventually outgrew even its unwilling hostess. And out of that malignancy grew Anna.

Funny, I didn't believe Buzzard when she first told me about Anna, but I had no trouble at all accepting the diagnosis of cancer. Cancer is incredibly persuasive, ultimately convincing.

"Surely there's a cure, some treatment," I remember saying.

"Cancer's the cure," Buzzard retorted flatly. "It's probably the cure for lots of things ... schizophrenia, acne ... it's definitely the cure for excess body fat, but as for a cure for cancer, *my* cancer ... forget it. I tried chemotherapy for a while after Anna was born. Not quite the quick fix I anticipated, though it's a great way to intimidate unwanted body hair." She ripped her soft silken helmet away, revealing a smooth, hairless head. "It's supposed to grow back, now that I cut the chemo out, but I rather like it. I've always wanted prominent cheekbones."

Buzzard held her face between her palms as though clasping a fragile cut-glass bowl — beautiful but hollow, and bound, inevitably, to break.

"But, Buzzard—"

"Honey, don't," she said softly. "I'm dying, and that's a fact. It's not so bad, I mean ... it doesn't hurt or anything."

"Buzzard!" I couldn't help it. I started to cry.

"Come on," she said lightly, re-covering her scalp. "Look at the bright side. It's given me a great idea for your next book — a digest of cancer jokes. You know, deathbed humor? Here's one. A priest came into my hospital room and offered me a mass, but I said, 'No, thanks. I already have one.'"

I stared at her incredulously.

"Sorry. I'm sure that was in bad taste, but I had to do something to get that funeral parlor expression off your face. Everybody dies ... I'm going to, you're going to. And in a way I'm lucky. I've had time to think about it ... to get used to the idea and make arrangements, throw away incriminating letters, clean out my drawers, choose a life for my kid."

The kid. Anna. For a moment I'd forgotten all about her.

Buzzard told me then, in a calm and conspiratorial whisper, that even her pubic hair had taken flight. She chuckled low in her throat and looked at me frantically, the desperate, darting stare of a wild bird, caged, pleading.

What the hell could I say?

"Gee," Buzzard faltered, "I oughta look up the lesbians. Bet they'd love it."

"I love you, Buzzard." For once in my life I'd stumbled upon the right thing to say. I held her close and our laughter soared, if only temporarily.

Later on it wasn't so easy. Buzzard began to hurt, in a big way. She lived out her days befuddled by the medication, barely managing the pain, her sharp wit vanquished, her pallor intensified by the stark reflection of hospital white. She didn't know where she was half the time, and her breath reeked of death. Cancer rendered her less than attractive, and when her eyes flew open for the last time, it was a blessed relief, agonizingly slow in coming.

✳

Of course I agreed to take Anna. What else could I do?

"The doctors here insisted that I terminate the pregnancy," Buzzard explained to me, in a frenzy of acute consciousness very near the end. "They couldn't begin to treat the cancer with Anna inside of me. That's why I went to Europe ... so I could have the child."

"Damned considerate of you," I said wretchedly, squeezing her hand.

"You bet," she said. "After all we've been to each other..."

I flinched, holding tightly to my tears. "And all we could have been."

Abruptly, she laughed.

"Our timing was lousy, that's all," Buzzard went on breathlessly, her words racing against the ravenous jowls of death yawning just behind her head. "Don't feel too badly about it. Just promise me that you'll take care of Anna. I love you both, so dearly, and can't bear the thought of leaving either one of you all alone."

54

"I promise," I wept, and held her, too desperately, too late. I felt her spirit shrink a bit, slipping elusively through the useless circle of my arms, backing away from me on tiptoe.

"Run toward the light, my darling," I whispered, and loved her enough to watch her go.

SHUBOP'S SAGA

WICKIE STAMPS

Shubop's memorial was well attended. The wake, organized by her lesbian co-workers from the newspaper, had the appropriate progressive trappings — there was a dash of people of color and a pinch of leather types, plus plenty of sobbing and wailing. Eulogies — antiracist and working-class in orientation — bemoaned the loss of Shubop to the women's community. The editors, worried that they wouldn't meet their weekly quota of "colorful" visuals, directed their photographers to get lots of shots of the gays and lesbians of color. And, since the paper was "pro-leather," they had already decided that Shubop's demise would be front-page news, and a snapshot of her in full leather would accompany the story.

Off to the side of this pristine farewell gathering hung a different set of rather pissed bereaved. Their ostracism to the nearby hill was self-imposed. This bunch of misfits and malcontents — streetwalkers, young queens with caps akimbo, and irritable drag queens — were the true friends of the dearly departed. More boring in both their attire and antics were the Communists, who had stood about looking oh-so-serious. The straight boys, most of whom were recovering addicts and fresh out of prison, elbowed for space amongst this mob. There were even feminists — older than those by the memorial site — who for years had hung in during Shubop's turn to sadomasochism. Shubop's sisters, Nell and Marfy, originally escorted directly to her memorial site, had intuitively meandered over and joined this crowd.

Flopped in the middle of this clump of ne'er-do-wells was Punkin — the departed's lover. She was a plump woman-child complete with garishly colored fingernails, red pouty lips, and John Belushi sunglasses. For the past hour she'd been picking her teeth, blaring her radio, and swatting at any consolation that her more foolhardy comrades offered.

"Cunts, jive-ass motherfucking bitches ... I should slap the shit out of them!" snarled this young thing. "If it wasn't for those whores at that jack-shit newspaper, Shubop would still be alive." She would occasionally interrupt this verbiage to take a drag on her cigarette and spit in the direction of the group that surrounded Shubop's memorial site. When the "bitchers and moaners" (as she'd nicknamed them) filed by, Punkin kick-started her Harley, which vomited up a billow of pollutants into their airspace. At least *something's* going my way today! she thought.

As she peeled off toward home, her mind quickly slid back to her life with Shubop, who was not only her lover but also her top and the co-parent of their cantankerous scaredy-cat, Ms. Squeak. Punkin had seen Shubop around the community for years but had figured that Shubop would never be interested in a young street urchin. Wrong. Shubop, who had been scoping Punkin out for months, was totally taken with the defiant, provocative munchkin. She'd taken

57

note of Punkin's fanny as she tinkered over her motorcycle, had checked Punkin out while she hung with her gay buddies, and was captivated by this young thing who was swishing about the community looking as fine and sassy as could be. Shubop even got a kick out of how Punkin had emulated the gay boys right down to 501 jeans with the bottom fly-button open.

Shubop, twenty years Punkin's senior, was often needled by her associates for this new taste for "chicken." But, true to form, Shubop told them all to "fuck off," and one evening at the local pool hall she had walked right up to Punkin, interrupted her winning shot, and asked her to take her home. And she did.

That was the start of two years of hot sex, sassy talk, and gentle romance. Shubop and Punkin were infamous for their tempestuous love affair. When they were bickering, everybody ducked. When they'd make up — which they always did — friends on all sides sighed with relief, for it meant they didn't have to listen to Shubop and Punkin denounce each other. Punkin, who had fought long and hard to drag herself out of the gutter, didn't take any shit from her Shubop. When Shubop pulled any of her crap — like grabbing Punkin's ass or sliding her hand up her dress — Punkin would tell her to get lost. Punkin demanded that Shubop treat her "like a lady." Punkin also laid down the law about Shubop's hot temper. So when Shubop got evil-tempered, she took it elsewhere. Everyone was grateful that these two, who had been so banged around by life, had hooked up. There was nothing like watching rough trade turn tender.

Since meeting Shubop, Punkin had rolled over into a femme. Originally nicknamed Spike, Punkin, who was right out of the projects, had, despite her momma's efforts, turned hard and had started running the streets, thieving and turning tricks at an early age. Before taking up with Shubop,

Punkin had actually leaned more toward a juvenile male street hustler than a young girl. But, since Shubop, Punkin had let her short spiked hair with the orange ponytail grow into a long black mane, complete with hair combs and ribbons. Shubop, who liked to think of Punkin as her slut (and nobody else's), was always talking trash to her, bringing her flowers and making her feel special. Sometimes — when she'd sit still long enough — Punkin would even let Shubop paint her toenails (which Punkin proudly sported to her friends; God forbid if you'd laugh — she'd kill you!). Upon occasion, Shubop even attempted to cook for Punkin, but Punkin always bogarted her way into the kitchen and drove Shubop out onto the porch just to get her out of her hair (which was really where Shubop wanted to be anyway). Although you'd be hard pressed to get her to confess it, Punkin enjoyed cooking for her lover and tending to her neglected cat, Ms. Squeak.

Punkin had no idea how she'd ever replace Shubop as a sexual partner. Before Shubop, Punkin stuck mostly to one-night stands and would, just to take the edge off the moment, give blow jobs to straight guys. When Shubop, who had been into lesbian sex since she was in the children's home, first snagged Punkin into bed, she had no idea that Punkin had a hankering for leather. Punkin, the more experienced of the two, had had to teach Shubop to mix the tough with the tender. Shubop, once she put her pride in her pocket, learned quickly and became, in Punkin's words, the "safe-sex kitten in the family." Punkin surprised herself with how much she allowed (and wanted) Shubop to do to her. Just thinking about some of their lovemaking, their golden-shower sessions, their ass fucking, or their animal games, caused Punkin to space out on her motorcycle and drift into another driving lane.

As she crossed the bridge into Boston, Punkin sighed, remembering what a fluff her Shubop really was. At their apartment, Shubop, who played a "tough-guy" role like a pro, had two stuffed animals that she had christened "Mr. Bear" and "Mr. Dog," and she loved to chitchat with them. She had gotten so comfortable with Punkin, she didn't even mind her overhearing these chats. Punkin chuckled to herself, for she knew that if Shubop were still alive, she'd kill her for even thinking about her lover's gentleness.

Shubop thought she was a real con artist, too. Their menagerie of pets was the product of her conning ways. If there was a six-toed, cockeyed, bony bugger of any species within a mile of Shubop, she'd sniff it out, drag it home, stash it under the porch, and, once in their apartment, sweet-talk Punkin into letting her keep it. Shubop always won.

Life had gone on this way until, out of the blue, Shubop started prattling about working at the local gay and lesbian paper. She'd gotten it into her head that she was going to be a writer. Punkin, as well as Shubop's cronies, was shocked. None of Shubop's buddies could understand why the hell she wanted to work there, since the joint had a reputation for being wicked stuck-up. And who the hell read that damn paper anyway?

Did it occur to Shubop that she might be out of her league? Nooooo. For Chris'sakes, she'd never even taken a grammar course, and when she *had* managed to stay in school, she was usually loaded on drugs. But did this faze Shubop? No way. She was going to write, and landing a job at the local gay and lesbian paper was a start, wasn't it? "Dumb cunt," thought Punkin as she quickly downshifted in order to outmaneuver some slowpoke driver.

But land a job at the paper she did. After ten thousand interviews, they hired her as their office manager. So off she went to that goddamn fucking newspaper. From day one, Punkin could smell disaster, for there was this small band of lesbians — not all of them, mind you — that Punkin knew would be nothing but trouble. Initially, these lesbians encouraged Shubop to voice her opinions, write stories, and help shape the political direction of the paper. When she disagreed with an article or a staff member's political position, she spoke her mind. She suggested topics, wrote articles, and submitted stories. But from jump street, something was wrong. Shubop didn't seem to know the right people. They took the list of contacts she suggested, thanked her politely, and never contacted a single one of them. Her ideas fell by the wayside. These women told their best friends about upcoming events, introduced them to the political leaders and artists who dropped into the office, and kept their cohorts posted on recently published books. But they always overlooked Shubop. Although she was seldom directly denied the option of writing a story, her articles were always cut, frequently held — and never made front page.

More often than not these lesbians informed Shubop that the paper's readership was probably not interested in what she thought would be interesting. She'd once told one of the editors that if anything came up on transvestites she'd be happy to cover it. That was two years ago. Shubop joked with her friends that the world of transvestites must be slow nowadays; otherwise, in the two years since that conversation, something newsworthy would have come across this editor's desk, right?

Most of the women at her job were terrified by Shubop's attitude and — with what Punkin could see — treated her like she was a nut case. Punkin had to admit that in looks and style Shubop could be rather intimidating. Punkin, who was very familiar with Shubop's bodaciousness, put it down to too many overamps on crystal Methedrine. And anyone who knew Shubop understood that, despite all her bravado and swearing, Shubop was a mush of a thing, had about as much self-confidence as a beaten dog, and was often more frightened of you than you were of her. Shubop had never hit anyone nonconsensually in her entire life but was, in fact, the one who had been slapped around for years — by men and women.

Also, Shubop was frightened by the way these girls at the paper snatched at issues like brass rings on a high-speed merry-go-round — and then, when they were bored of the issue, like spoiled children they'd toss the month's tarnished agony back into the lives of the people they'd stolen it from. In June, while the girls were indignant about foster care and parental rights, Shubop's belly was in knots as memories of her years in orphanages rushed at her. Then, in July, the girls swung into high gear over "women's health." During this phase, the young woman who was responsible for the collective's health coverage was so into writing a front-page article on women's health that she ignored the transfer of Shubop's health insurance from her previous job. When the young lesbian finally tended to her job, Shubop, who was considered high risk because of her history of IV drug use, was denied insurance. Needless to say, this "women's health issue" didn't warrant an article.

As Punkin skirted some of the rougher sections of the city, her thoughts meandered into Shubop's struggle with "women's health issues" that she was too ashamed to mention at the paper. Her twenty-year battle with drugs and booze had spanned both her heterosexuality and lesbianism. The girls at the paper didn't know Shubop had been in shelters, in low-bottom boardinghouses, and occasionally on the streets. The consequences of decades of abuse — teeth rotted from crystal Methedrine, untreated venereal disease — gnawed at her health. She never mentioned all the years she'd sat for hours in overcrowded public health clinics and dealt with staff who brazenly discussed your private business in front of everyone — all for a few shots of penicillin in the ass. When she'd finally get into an

62

examining room and the staff would walk out for a moment, she'd steal the prescription pads, rubber tubing, and (if lucky) hypodermic needles. Because if she'd come home empty-handed to her old man, a dope fiend and dealer, he would've kicked the shit out of her. "Women's health my ass!" hissed Punkin to herself as, blind with rage, she cut off a motorist whose looks got on her nerves.

Nowhere in the paper's pages, nor in their conversations, did Shubop's "type" of lesbianism crop up. Christ, on the planet Shubop came from, which apparently was not the same one as these women, she spent her days just trying not to get baited or bashed. With her short-cropped hair, tattoos, and leather jacket, she was a walking target for someone's unoccupied rage. She started her day by gingerly side-stepping the slurs spit at her by the gang of idle punks congregated on the porch next door.

When she came out — at thirty-three — Shubop spent a whole year (and a whole lot of money) trying to seduce her straight friend Alberta, who was an ex-dope fiend and retired hooker. The two would lay up at Alberta's getting blind on herb and Courvoisier. They could always scrape up enough change to send Alberta's boys to the fish truck. The kids would come back loaded down with fried catfish soaked in hot sauce and slapped between two slices of Wonder Bread. Even though Shubop paid the family's oil bills and wrote Alberta's college papers, she never got any play. Zip. But Alberta fed her, took her to bingo (for good luck), and flirted heartlessly with the lovesick Shubop. This coming-out tale — girl meets hooker — never hit her paper's pages.

Shubop, who had heard these women say that "closeting equaled co-optation," also never mentioned her closeted drug addict brother, Phonso, even though he'd sometimes call — drunk and frightened — during staff meetings. For years their daddy had beaten him because he wasn't "man enough" and would leave Phonso stranded at the Woolworth's where he worked and make him walk the ten miles home in the freezing rain — to make a man out of his faggot son. When things got bad enough, her brother would just slit his wrists — a family tradition. From what she heard at the paper, her brother and his story had nothing to do with gay and lesbian liberation. As Punkin drove down the side streets, her fists were wrapped so tightly around her handlebars that her knuckles ached. She flashed on Shubop waiting on "the call" she knew would come that would notify her that her brother had made the headlines — not on the cover of her gay paper but in the obits of some other paper someplace else.

It seemed that every time Shubop opened her mouth these young lesbians insinuated that she was a misogynist. Couldn't they see that women were Shubop's heart? First, there was her tough-skinned Irish momma who, when she wasn't in prison for drugs, single-handedly fed, clothed, and loved five kids. If you ran away from home, you ran to Shubop's momma. If you were shooting dope, she'd clean your abscesses and feed you TV dinners (which, for company, she took out of the foil trays and put on real plates). Shubop used to tell Punkin how proud she was of her momma, who, at age sixty, still flirted with gas station attendants and received silk stockings from her male admirers. "Not bad for an old broad," Shubop used to say. After her momma's overdose — which occurred while Shubop worked at the paper — Punkin had held Shubop every night for weeks while she mourned her loss.

Then there were Shubop's sisters — a couple of bawdy, flamboyant things. Punkin knew that when she was in their presence, she was treading on matriarchal turf. They doted on Shubop. From the time they were kids, they'd raised their "baby sister," Shubop. Not much older than Shubop herself, they'd each concocted their own angle on mothering and were always fixing her collar or rearranging her scarf. When Shubop came out as a lesbian, they continued to fuss over her. Nell, the oldest, would inspect Shubop like a drill sergeant and assert that "even if you insist on being a gawd-damned lesbian you will still dress properly."

When Shubop was down and out, Marfy, the one in the middle, would bring her "care packages" that were as inappropriate as their upbringing — grocery bags overflowing with caviar and smoked oysters. Shubop and Marfy had been in the children's home together. During their momma's incarceration, Nell would bust them out for the weekend and let them stay at her shabby apartment, where they'd stay up late eating as much noodles with gobs of butter as their bellies could take and terrifying themselves watching the creature double features. When times got hard for her at the paper, Shubop would drive out for a visit with Marfy and they'd reminisce about the children's home.

Punkin knew that Shubop did have some friends at the paper. There was her mentor, Boris, a talented, aging queen whose guidance lit her way into the gay world and the subculture of sadomasochists. Since meeting Boris, Shubop had checked out Bergman films and read about Rainer Fassbinder, Capote, and Warhol. By introducing her to writers and editors across the country, he was instrumental in launching her fledgling writer's career. A nationally recognized writer himself, he was an icon to a circle of young gay men and older lesbians, all of whom were writers. The members of this enclave became Shubop's pals. Boris would, in a beat-to-shit black leather biker's jacket (which clutched his generous belly like a surgical binder), stroll into the office and hold court with whoever was about. In his inimitable style he'd whip hilarious zingers at the entourage of lesbians who tortured Shubop — and himself. Shubop cherished their gossip sessions, for it was where she learned the weapons of camping and trashing.

Boris's crew — about ten in all — lived and breathed art, music, and politics. Marty (a.k.a. "Ms. Pris") was the upstart socialist of the brood. Dressed in baggy tweed jackets, khakis, and Hawaiian shirts, he looked like a twenties Bolshevik who'd gotten lost on the West Coast. He flirted shamelessly with Shubop. Then there was Willie, with droopy jeans and yellow hanky in his right back pocket, who, like Shubop, practiced sadomasochism. They'd sit around the office and compare notes on sexual practices and would jointly venture into the local leather shops, where they'd shop until they dropped. Both co-conspired against their lovers, who, they were convinced, mercilessly tortured and victimized them. Like Boris, Willie prodded Shubop to keep writing and publishing and, recognizing how ashamed she was of her choppy education, gently instructed her in grammar and spelling. From Willie, Shubop received minute-by-minute news flashes on — what else — the sex life of Madonna.

Shubop had also befriended Christine, one of the women staffers. She'd won Shubop's heart when she showed up at work in men's boxers that hung out below her Bermuda shorts. This hot-shit little dyke thought, like Shubop, that the whole kit and kaboodle of lesbians at the paper were "totally fucked."

Shubop had other survival tactics. On lunch breaks she might cut out and head into the gay ghetto, where she'd cruise the local trade or forage for a trinket for Punkin. Once a week Shubop would drop in on her pal Kara, a Native American S/M dyke who worked next door at the local homeless shelter. During these sessions, Shubop would get the standard pep talk. "Don't let those motherfuckers at that job get to you, do you hear me?" Kara would lecture, accenting her point with a charley horse to Shubop's arm.

Although every day had become an emotional horror show, Shubop's final staff meeting was a doozy. Shubop, who handled the paper's faltering finances, suggested the paper start taking credit cards. She asserted that credit cards would make it easier for people to buy subscriptions and advertising. One of the young lesbians — who had irked Shubop for months — took this moment to launch into an hour-long diatribe about "Plastic Money as the Cornerstone of Capitalism." Shubop lost it. She pulled out her switch-blade, whizzed it into the table between her and the pontificating party and, before the blade stopped twanging, whipped off a score of "motherfuckers," "cunts," and "bitches." Shubop concluded her show by pointing out that the "pompous bitch" had no fucking qualms using her daddy's credit cards to fly around the country, now did she? Total disaster.

Willie screamed and jumped up onto his chair; Ms. Pris suddenly looked very interested in his tofu soup; and Christine almost pissed her boxer shorts (although secretly everyone was thrilled at this fiasco, for their gossip lines — all of which fed into control central manned by Boris — had, of late, suffered a drought).

Shubop then grabbed her leather jacket, stormed out of the office, and split, full throttle, on her motorcycle. The next news of her came from the state police who, shortly there-after, had found Shubop's motorcycle shattered on the rocks by the ocean. They dragged the waters but never found the body. All assumed the current had taken it out to sea.

Remembering these last few days, Punkin gritted her teeth and frantically blinked her eyes to hold back the rage, tears, and sobs. Arriving home, she dismounted her bike, tugged off her gloves, and began to slowly mount the stairs to their apartment. She wondered why Ms. Squeak, who always perched in the window, wasn't at her designated outpost. As she put the key into her apartment door Punkin was yanked inside and slammed full force into a very familiar chest.

It was Shubop! Punkin was shocked, then thrilled, then megapissed. She wrenched herself from Shubop's hug. "You're alive!" she hissed. "You son of a bitch ... you..." She started banging on Shubop's chest while Shubop just roared with laughter and messed up Punkin's girly hairdo.

"That's right, sugarbeet. I wanted revenge. So, I figured, if those witches thought they'd sent me to my grave, they'd be devastated — or at least a little guilty." She snorted. "Anyway I finally got my name on the front page of that fucking newspaper, now didn't I?" By this point Punkin had leaped onto Shubop, knocked her onto the bed ... and they were off and running.

CACTUS LOVE

LEE LYNCH

Until that night, I'd have bet my bottom dollar I was a washout. It'd been ten years since I'd touched my last woman in love. Too much like walking barefoot onto a sprawling prickly pear cactus in the dark. I just didn't have the energy for love.

Then Van came, with her youth and her brains. I hired her to run the retail end of my cactus ranch. That left me free to spend all my time on the growing, the watering, and — well, I ran out of things to do. I'd watch that young body run around, enjoying the heck out of life. Even after her breakup with Ivy she was back in the saddle before you could say Jack Rabbit.

That was October. I can still see her standing in the bright sunlight outside my trailer, one foot on the metal step, saying, "I'm going down to the bar tonight. Want to bet I find a lover before Christmas?" What'd she do then? Went out and got one. I confess that girl's been an inspiration to me. I went out and got one too.

Whoopee! I feel like dancing with my cactuses.

Billie is older than me by a couple of years, but she doesn't look like anybody's cute little grandma. Van called her The Matriarch, from the way the young ones at the bar would chew her ear.

I watched Billie.

I liked looking at her, sitting straight as a ruler's edge at the bar. She's part Irish, part Zuni Indian; tall, but very skinny. Her bones are so broad and strong-looking you'd think she was some desert wild thing. Maybe that's what put me off at first. I'd always been one for younger, femmier types. But Billie, she's beyond all that. She's not butch, not femme. She's no garden variety female at all. She's a monument. I could listen to her talk about her life all night—

But it wasn't listening I did that first night.

She had about as much stomach for that smoky, loud joint with its watered-down country jukebox as I did. She always left around eleven, just before it got real loud and wild. I'd decided after the first few times I saw her that I wanted at least to talk to her. The next time I went to the bar, though, I dithered and dithered. Before I knew it, it was eleven o'clock and she was leaving and I couldn't think of a blamed thing to say to her anywhere as good as "Would you like to dance?" I'd missed my chance. So I let it go another week.

But you know, she started coming into my head a lot that week. When I was in bed at night I'd imagine her, with that long, strong body next to me on the white sheets. I could imagine the life story she'd tell. And I could imagine her hands on me; I'd noticed them when I was next to her at the bar ordering drinks. The beginnings of arthritis: a little stiffness, knobbiness. Still, you got the feeling that that bit of bother would be as likely to stop her as spines stop birds from nesting in a cactus. I could feel the seasoned fingers on my hip, and on the other parts of me that were never this cushiony for my earlier girlfriends. I kind of just ran her through my head, to see if I'd like it, or if I only wanted her because we were close in age. I'd get wiggly at the thought of Billie's touch. Not many women can seep into my head like she did, in the dark.

So the next Saturday night, that lulu of a night, I asked her to dance. She looked down at me and said nothing, nothing at all. But there was a little smile that puckered the corner of her mouth. And those brown eyes like polished jasper looked like they were laughing. Then she swept me out onto the dance floor. Swept me out there and danced me around those young couples like she'd put me on wheels. I'd never felt so light on my feet. That darned woman took my breath away. I never wanted the dance to end.

I asked her back to our table. Van was sweet-talking her lover-to-be, so they didn't pay us much attention. Luckily it'd taken me till ten-thirty to get up the nerve to buttonhole Billie. By this time it was getting on toward eleven and noisy. I told her about my business, asked her if she'd ever seen a cactus ranch by moonlight.

"Well, no," she said, laughing. "I can't say that I have, or heard such a barefaced line."

She lived near the bar and didn't have a vehicle. I drove her out here in Pickup Nellie, my old white Chevy. We parked behind one of the hothouses. Wonder of wonders, there was a moon shining down. Not quite full, but full enough. The moon looked like it was pounding up there, in time to my heart. The night was pretty darned hot for November.

We walked out on the desert a ways, without a flashlight. She was wordless, quiet-moving. I was just enjoying the company, come what may. Big patches of yellow desert broom like earth moons glowed at our feet. We didn't go too far so as not to disturb any critters.

On the way back, she took my hand. I thought I'd melt right there at her feet, like some little teenaged person.

"You want to come in?" I asked when we reached my trailer house.

"I didn't come all this way to turn around now," she replied, her teeth white against that sunburnt-looking skin. There was a dogtooth missing. I thought of her moist tongue seeking out the empty spot, all alone inside her mouth. Holy Toledo, I knew I was a goner when ideas like that crept up on me.

Billie squints when she talks, like she's measuring you. "I've been noticing you at the bar," she said, over some ice coffee I threw together. "You're not my type at all."

I had to grin. "You're not mine either."

She nodded. "If there's one thing I have learned in my life, it's that you have to take things as they come. It doesn't do to fight your spirit, it always gets its way. If it wants to go changing my tastes in women at the ripe old age of sixty-nine, well then, I'm ready."

"Same here," I said. "I never wanted another girlfriend. All that heartache. But—" And I told her about Van's coming, and about the blood that got stirred up in my veins. "I could take the lonesomes," I told her, "till I started wanting again."

"I hear you. I sit in my little cement-block apartment and tell myself I'll stay home with the cat, read a good book, watch the TV. I don't need that bar. It's not the liquor that calls me; half the time I order milk, trying to put some flesh on these bones." She lifted her arm like I could see the scrawniness under her striped jersey. "Maybe I feel useful there. The kids come and pour their little hearts out to me. Sometimes they think they want to get me into bed, but, to

72

tell the truth, their energy drives me up a wall. I'd never get any peace."

She paused, setting down her glass. "I'm thinking, little Windy Sands, maybe I could stand a change of pace."

I told you the lady was big. Those arms were long. She reached clear across my narrow tabletop. Now her eyes were like some wise bird's looking into mine for I don't know what, for some kind of sign, I suppose. Then she kissed me, a little shakily from that distance, her hands kneading my shoulders. And I kissed her back, giving her everything I had to let her know it wasn't just the kids who wanted her.

I stood and led her to the bedroom, still with her hands on my shoulders, like she couldn't find her way without me.

"I guess we both know what comes next," I said, laughing. "But I'll keep the light out if you don't mind."

"Why? Because you've got an old body?" she asked. "Hell, it's not even as old as mine!"

"Yeah, but you're slender as the needles on a pinyon pine."

"I'm skinny, you mean. And I have scars."

She switched the light on. I saw the scars. An artery taken out of her leg for heart trouble. Gut trouble where she'd been sliced open a couple of times. That took my mind off me: I was whole, even with this body round and pale as another earth moon.

We lay full out against each other, as if we were hungry. As if we were on fire and thought that by pressing ourselves together we could put it out.

We held like that for a long time. It felt *so* good, but it didn't put out my fire. The longer we held, the hotter I felt. I wondered if the same thing was happening to Billie, but knew I wouldn't find out till I reached between her legs, and it was too soon for that, old hands at this stuff or not.

After a while I started rubbing and rubbing against her, just the way we were, pressed together. She kissed me again, and I smelled the ice coffee and felt her sweat and the heat of our bodies in the trailer's hot air. Her skin felt slick, and marked like the moon. We kissed and pressed into each other. Then, swift as a crafty old rock dweller looking for shade, she wriggled her arm between us. Oh, she found out I was raring to go. I heard her exhale. I don't know for sure that she was excited before then, but hot-ziggety if that didn't do it for her.

She took her lips from mine and started kissing and licking my neck and my face, her tongue in my ear, in my mouth. I rode the heel of her hand like she was some fine horse taking me out across the desert under the blue blue Arizona sky, taking me up a mountainside, green and lush like it gets over on the east end of Tucson. We rode so fast I could hear the leaves stir from our passage until the sound of a rushing waterfall began to grow. She stopped so I could see, so I could feel, so I *was* that water falling from the mountain. Falling down and down and down and—

Ten years of bottled-up pleasure. Everything spilled out of me.

What I said, after that, was, "I'm too darned exhausted to turn over. Can we talk for a while?"

"Sure thing, Windy. If you have the breath to talk. Was that too much for you?"

"Not enough," I panted. "Not hardly enough, Billie."

It was the first time I heard that laugh of hers — the mysterious-sounding, low, back-of-the-throat laugh that reminds me of Frank Sinatra singing about "come-hither looks" in my younger days.

She began then, telling me about the places where she had been raised in New Mexico. I tried to listen, but sleep came over me like a red-tailed hawk onto a tasty pocket gopher. All I recall is that it got too cold nights up there in the mountains for her. She migrated south in her truck and got factory work where she could. Now she's retired.

I was out long enough for the moon to follow us to my bedroom, right inside the trailer window. Billie was asleep too.

Oh, the moonlight on that body. Billie was less than slender, she was as bony as an ancient saguaro turned brown and ribby. Hips, shoulders, ribcage, and all made her like a cradle I just fit into. My hand waltzed over the juts and hollows of her. I felt weak — from exertion? Lust? Maybe all I needed was a little snack.

No. I couldn't leave the sight before me, the white moonlight on the deep-toned body. She was handsome as all get out.

It didn't take long for one of my caresses to wake her. She opened her eyes and her mouth and groaned for me. I just plunged in then, wondering if she'd ever had babies, she was so big. Plunged one finger, then two, then a third. She made herself smaller around me. I was too short to reach up and kiss her. She was too hot to bend down to me. I rested my cheek on her breast, plunged harder, deeper, softer, slower, quicker. She brought her hands flat across my shoulders and drummed and drummed and drummed as she came.

"If I smoked," she said after a while, "I'd say that calls for a cigarette."

"Cigarette, nothing. A ten-gun salute!"

We decided to settle for my snack.

She sat up all grins, like a little kid going to a party. We padded to the kitchen bare-assed, dragged every darn thing out of that icebox we could find, and had ourselves a feast.

Billie didn't stop beaming during the whole meal.

What am I talking about? Looking at the gap in her teeth, the mussed gray hair, and those brown eyes like mirrors full

75

of desert roads and pickup trucks, honky-tonk gay bars and jukebox-dancing women, full of sixty-nine years of love and disappointment and love again, ah, jeeze, I knew I'd found somebody who was going to make all the mess and bother of love worthwhile — and I'm still grinning right back at her to this day.

TEAMWORK

LUCY JANE BLEDSOE

The first thing any of us noticed about Thalia Peterson was her legs. And I mean *legs*. To top it off, the girl could play ball.

We all knew when she joined the team there'd be changes. Not that we were blatant about anything. But when you work out together three to four hours a day — and I do mean *together,* because good basketball is teamwork — you get to reading each other intimately. But you don't go talking about it. So we all knew who liked girls, who did it with boys, who hated white girls, and who thought black people were dumb. We had all those kinds of people on the team. But on a good ball team you learn to respect each other's ball playing and that's how you relate — around ball. And you become so tightly woven into each other's lives just by so much sweat, wins and losses, fights and tears, and midgame highs, that you can have all your homophobia, heterophobia, racism, and what have you and still not be able to separate yourself from your teammates. On the court, anyway.

Thalia Peterson was this southern white girl — big-legged, with big white teeth, and a thick ponytail of the smoothest blonde hair you ever saw. The thing that tipped me off right away were her eyes. They were both narrow-set and deep-set at the same time. The lashes were dark and long, and the eyes themselves, pretty as they were, were not very big. They got me, 'cause she seemed farther back there than most people. Like, I was wondering if we'd ever be able to read her like we read one another. Then, too, she wore makeup. Not that we weren't used to that. Both Kathy Jones and Amanda Severson wore makeup, and of course that was their business. But Thalia's makeup was straight out of *Glamour* magazine, almost a lifestyle. She had the kind of looks boys made a point of turning and looking at, because if they didn't their manhood would be questioned. Me, I knew she was pretty. But her looks weren't the kind I fell for. Just couldn't stomach those eyes.

Thalia Peterson was a junior, like me. She'd been at the university for two years, but hadn't come out for the team. End of her freshman year she pledged Phi Beta Pi, the snottiest sorority on campus, and got herself established there before revealing her jock talents. That was her business, of course, though some say she waited two years just so she could blow everyone away when she *did* come out for the team.

Anyway, at first we kind of liked her sorority connections, because suddenly our home-game crowds swelled full of her Phi Beta Pi sisters and their fraternity boyfriends. The fact was, people *loved* to watch Thalia Peterson play ball, and I couldn't blame them. She was a big girl, strong and tall, and damn near the most aggressive ball player I've ever seen. Get up under that basket for a rebound and *boom!* she'd block you out by throwing her powerful behind into you, more often than not sending you flying across the floor. She never got fouls called on her, neither, because the refs couldn't believe someone that feminine and pretty had any *umph*. You could see a quick puzzled look cross the ref's face before he decided that Thalia's opponent must have just fallen down. *She* couldn't've pushed that girl on the floor. Truth was, in addition to a well-aimed elbow, Thalia Peterson was very skilled in getting her body in the right place at the right time.

There was something else about Thalia Peterson: She didn't just like winning. She expected to win, even *lived* to win — in everything.

Most women on the team didn't enjoy her as much as the fans in the audience did. They didn't think it fair for her to come out for the team her junior year when the rest of us had struggled up from junior varsity since our freshman year. I didn't see that it mattered. But then she didn't bump my position, either. I didn't have much of a position. I came off the bench as a guard when the game was clearly won or clearly lost. That was okay with me. Games scared me shitless. I played for the practices, the uniforms, the feeling of being on a team. But some people cared a great deal about Thalia Peterson coming out her junior year. Kathy Jones, for one. And Carson McDuffy, for another. Kathy Jones I already told you wore makeup, was real skinny and gangly, and played center mostly. She was a fantastic shooter and rebounder, but sometimes inconsistent and definitely a bad ball handler. Carson McDuffy was hot. She could do everything — dribble, pass, shoot, and sometimes even rebound, though she was only five foot four. Her problem was that she played forward, insisted on it, in spite of her height. Her other problem was that she was hotheaded.

Carson was a very serious-minded ball player, hilarious off the court, singular in her likes and dislikes (luckily, I was one of her likes), and a lesbian. She had a medium-sized, angular body, short brown hair, and sallow white skin. Scruffy described her most of the time. Carson had her goals set on making the Eastern Division All-Star team.

On the first day of tryouts for the university team that fall, Carson's confidence glowed. She made passes behind her back, crashed through a crowded key for lay-ups, and fast-broke the rest of us to death.

"Okay," I told her. "So you've been working out all summer. Easy on the rest of us, okay?"

She fired me one of her try-and-stop-me grins and pressed harder. The truth was, she'd never looked better. The rest of us always took her with a grain of salt, she was so crazy. But her enthusiasm spurred us on. I hoped almost as much as she did that she'd make the Eastern Division All-Star team this year.

Carson noticed Thalia Peterson during tryouts, all right. And she planned on putting her in her place immediately. When Coach Montgomery shouted, "Pair up for one-on-one," Carson made her move. I saw her cock her finger, thumb up, at Thalia. "You," was all she said. Then she strode toward Thalia as if she was coming on to her. "Oh, god," I said under my breath. That woman always reminded me of lit dynamite that never quite explodes.

By instinct, the rest of us backed off the court to watch. Carson shot a bullet pass at Thalia's middle. "You go first," she said. Thalia caught the pass as gracefully as if it had been lobbed. Even before Montgomery blew the whistle, Carson's hands were working Thalia, cutting the air before her face like blades. Thalia maintained a regal stance, casual and disinterested. The whistle blew. Thalia faked a jump shot, then moved left. Carson stayed on her, grinning and chattering like a monkey. "Go ahead, go ahead," she threatened. "Try and get around me. Try."

Thalia tried, her blonde ponytail swinging back and forth on her back. When she couldn't get past Carson she

80

stopped, figuring she could easily put up a jump shot over Carson's head.

Shouting a loud war cry, Carson stuffed the attempted shot. She wiped her hands on her shorts, chased down the ball, and stood at the top of the key waiting for Montgomery's whistle. That's when I first noticed how much Thalia hated to lose. She was *mad*. But she wore her anger like a queen, chin up and eyes smoldering like rubies. Even so, Carson drove by her for three fast breaks in a row. And after each goal, Carson hooted her triumph in hyenalike howls as she trotted back up to the top of the key.

The fourth time, she missed the lay-up and Thalia rebounded. It was her game after that. She'd miscalculated Carson's talents, but now that she knew them, she could meet them. Thalia faked left, drove right, stopped short, and popped a jump shot. Next she sunk a rimless goal from the top of the key, right over Carson's hands. To prove she could drive, Thalia pushed to the left, lost Carson as she cut under the basket, and hooked the ball in. At that point Coach sent Carson to the locker room for cursing out loud, and Thalia toweled the back of her neck, easy and casual. Her every gesture said it was nothing.

After that day, we knew Carson hated Thalia and some of us wondered if she'd quit the team if Thalia got her starting position. The other starters were Stella Robinson at forward, Kathy Jones at center, and Susan Thurmond and Jackie Sanchez (who I was at the time beginning to fall deeply in something with) at guards. Now, Stella Robinson was a cool woman and she didn't get ruffled at much of anything. She wouldn't be threatened by Thalia anyway, because Stella was tall, strong, and consistent. Besides, she didn't care if she sat the bench some. Stella was together, her own woman.

Everyone knew that Stella was sleeping with our coach, Hilary Montgomery, and nobody saw any need to do much more than raise an eyebrow. It would be one thing if Stella were no good and Montgomery were playing her all the time. But fact was, Stella was key to our team — smooth, consistent, just what hotheaded Carson needed out there to shine. So Coach and Stella were together and it was their business. They kept it to themselves. If any of us were interested, we kept *that* to *our*selves.

Well, sure enough, the season started and Thalia wound up bumping Carson mostly. No one really blamed Montgomery, except Carson. Carson had been a star, all right, but she was too short and had needed a lot of setting up. Thalia could set herself up. And besides, without Carson out there turning cartwheels to the basket, Stella was freer to show off her stuff, and she did. With Thalia on the team, we stood a chance of going to the play-offs. What made me mad, though, was the tiny glint of triumph way back in those cryptic eyes of Thalia's. That wasn't necessary, and I just knew it made Carson's blood boil like magma in the core of the earth.

Teams always have a lot of tension on them. Sometimes the tension is the main thing holding them together. But Thalia's presence brought a new kind of tension that we couldn't handle in our usual way. She seemed to almost control us. The locker room after practice lost its jocular, towel-slapping, good-time feeling. A lot of people think jocks are immature, but I think there's something hotly primal about being naked in a locker room after having sprinted for three hours, being all sweaty, and the place being all steamed up from hot showers. God, I'm never happier than I am then. But with Thalia there, everything changed. I got the feeling she didn't like to undress in front of us. Yet, because of some kind of pride, she walked around, thrusting out her round belly, ass, and breasts, as if to make it clear that no lesbians were gonna cow her. We all averted our eyes, too. Not that I *wanted* to look. I didn't. But a dangerous heterosexual energy wafted off her like power-ful perfume.

Most of us cooled down, pulled on our pants, joked about dinner. Basketball practice launched me into the rest of my life, like it was the source and everything else flowed from there. But for Thalia, the locker room was a place of transition. She had a routine as amazing as a Dr. Jekyll–and–Mr. Hyde act. As she applied makeup and pulled on nylon stockings, she slowly transformed from basketball animal to Phi Beta Pi lady. She often shaved her legs in the locker room, slowly and carefully, as if to show how much the rest of us needed to do the same. By the time she left the locker room, this basketball powerhouse had become the most graceful swan you ever saw.

So the locker room was a lot quieter that year. We just showered and went off to dinner. Team jokes from last year fell flat and no new ones arose. Something about Thalia made me feel young and inadequate. Only Stella seemed to be at ease with her, making small conversation with her as if she didn't notice Thalia's cool response. Thalia was too southern polite not to speak when spoken to, but she didn't want to talk, that was clear. We all saw that and didn't try. Except Stella.

I admired Stella more than anyone on the team. She was so solid. Jackie told me that Stella went to church every Sunday morning. She struck you as beautiful when you first saw her because of her carriage, but on closer look her face was rather plain. At first I didn't get why she was with Coach. Montgomery was a 35-year-old white woman from the Midwest. She had broad, even features and a jaunty smile — *when* she smiled, which wasn't often. She was a good coach, but I thought a dull person. Stella was a black woman from L.A. In a way, though black and white, Stella and Mont-gomery looked a bit alike. The big difference besides color was Stella's elegance and Montgomery's jock walk. The two of them were pretty discreet, because much as I tried I never saw anything pass between them during practices. They must have, at times, been scared. I sure was, and I didn't have a job to protect.

I wasn't religious, but I privately drew from Stella's sure confidence. I wasn't brave, either, but I drew from Montgomery's courage to live and love as she pleased. Without speaking an intimate word with either of these two women, I considered them my lesbian mentors. As something nameless thickened between Jackie and myself, I kept my eyes trained on Montgomery and Stella, looking for a signal, the go-ahead, something in their plain, forward-moving faces that would tell me what my next move should be.

✳

On the night of our third home game, as I jogged out onto the court with my team, I was so happy I thought I could die right then and be satisfied with my life. Jackie and I had finally started up our love affair. A sweetness coursed through my limbs, making me feel like an Olympic hurdler flying over life's obstacles with perfect elegance. On top of that, our team was winning. Our record was a tremendous 7–0. Thalia's family donated brand-new uniforms to the team (she had been complaining all season about how ghastly ugly the old ones were), so we were looking pretty good, too. When we lined up for lay-ups the school band blasted into action. Even the cheerleading squad pranced onto center court and whipped their pom-poms around. Understand that the band and cheerleaders did not attend women's games until we were on a winning streak, until there was glory to be reaped. I wasn't bitter, though. I loved it. I even loved the hordes of fraternity boys that packed the gym. The night was fine.

We were playing North Carolina State, and we held a decent lead during most of the first half. I sat back on the bench and watched Jackie speed up and down the court. The movement of each muscle was a precious sight to me.

Shortly before halftime, Montgomery benched Thalia to give her a breather and put in Carson. Suddenly, the game turned around. North Carolina State broke our lead and then, in a quick ten minutes, proceeded to fast-break themselves to an eight-point lead. Seconds before halftime, North Carolina State got the ball again, and went for the fast break. The guard tipped the ball in for a lay-up just as the halftime buzzer sounded. The official called the basket good. Montgomery lunged onto the court toward the ref, screaming that the basket sunk *after* the buzzer.

The ref slapped his hand to the back of his head, pointed at Montgomery, and called a tech on her. The crowd went crazy, because Montgomery was right. That girl wasn't anywhere near the basket when the buzzer sounded. But someone pulled Montgomery back on the bench, and we lined up at half court while the player toed the line for her free throw. Carson was kicking the floor like a mad bull, because she knew everyone would interpret our sudden slide as a result of Montgomery putting her in and taking Thalia out. The North Carolina State player made her shot.

After a good talking to at halftime, we trotted back out onto the court and warmed up. Then Montgomery did something that surprised us all. She started Carson instead of Thalia. I figured she thought Carson was losing her confidence and so put her in there to let her know she wasn't to blame for the score. Montgomery always emphasized that we were a *team,* that one woman couldn't make or break anything.

A nervous silence fell on the gym as the ten players took positions for the tip-off. A cold sweat saturated the air. I could see Carson's mouth working and would have thought that she was praying if I didn't know better. Jackie wiped her hands on her hips and glanced at me. I felt instant warmth again. The ref held the ball up and glanced around the circle. He hesitated as two players suddenly traded places. Then, just as he bent his knees to make the toss, a male voice in the bleachers erupted like a geyser out of the perfect silence: "Bench the dyke! Play Thalia Peterson."

For a split second, everyone in the gym was stunned. The air felt yellow and still, like in the eye of a storm. Even the ref, who stood between the two centers with the ball balanced on his fingertips, stepped back and squinted up in the stands for a moment. Then a gurgling of fraternity laughter eased some people's discomfort, and the ref tossed the ball.

Something turned sour for me in that moment at halftime against North Carolina State. Everyone knew the fraternity boy meant Carson, but I also knew that he meant Stella and Montgomery, Jackie and myself. The raw hatred in that boy's voice felt like a boot stomping on a tender green shoot.

We lost that game and the next one, too. Every time I stepped into the big, silent gym for practice, I would hear an echo of that boy's voice. Sometimes, for a flashing second, I could even see the group of fraternity boys in the stands, jeering, *knowing*. Montgomery and Stella were no help any more; they were as indicted as I. Jackie and I had our first fight that week.

Looking back, I think it's a miracle we ever won any games. So many of us were in some stage of coming out, no one really comfortable, none of us able to say "lesbian" without cringing. We were scared, we were in love, we were all little bundles of explosive passion. Sometimes this energy fairly drove us to victory on the court; other times we crumbled under it.

By midseason Jackie and I were solid. We were crazy for each other. But love isn't everything. We fought constantly. She didn't know what she was doing messing with a white girl, and I didn't know what I was doing messing with any girl at all. Our common ground lay in the realm of ideals and primal loves and fears. But our earthbound experiences were different enough to drive us both crazy. We loved each other and we drove one another to fierce anger. But we carried on, just the same.

After the North Carolina State game, Montgomery began switching around the starting lineup. It's not like she substituted one starter for another (say, Carson for Thalia), but out of the top six players she tried different combinations and often Carson was in there. Sometimes Thalia was not.

Mixing up the starting lineup too much might not be smart basketball (though in this case it might have been), but it sure made me like Montgomery. I don't really know why she did it, but I suspect she saw it as a morale issue. She probably noticed how that boy's remark registered on some of our young faces. Maybe she knew she had some power to erase the imprint of that boot. With me, she was right. I secretly drew from her strength like an invisible leech. But the morale of the rest of the team sagged.

When Thalia didn't start, she lounged on the bench as if it were a settee, as if she was entertaining in a drawing room and hadn't the faintest interest in the game. And when Montgomery put her in, she gave only seventy-five percent. If Montgomery started her, however, Thalia gave her all. The insult to Montgomery, even the *idea* that she could be manipulated by Thalia's insolence, infuriated me. I was glad when Montgomery started her less and less often. A rumor circulated that Thalia's parents offered a large donation to the women's intercollegiate fund on the behind-closed-doors stipulation that Thalia be reinstated as a permanent first stringer. I don't really know if this was true, but people swore it was. Someone knew someone who knew someone who worked in Dean Roper's office. She'd *heard* the offer. I believed the story more than I disbelieved it.

Carson saw the changing lineup as an opportunity to re-establish her position on the team. Her attitude improved. She kept her mouth shut and played ball like it was a matter of life and death. At the same time, Carson became more and more out about her lesbianism. And she thought everyone else should come out as well. "A bunch of fucking closet dykes," she semi-joked at me and Jackie one night in the library. She took that boy's word like it was a piece of clay and fashioned her own meaning out of it. Still, I cringed and quickly looked over my shoulder to see if anyone was within earshot. Jackie just shrugged. "With Montgomery and Stella, we're talking about a job," she said. Yeah, I thought. And for me, we're talking about fear. Jackie didn't want to come out, and I happily hid behind her wishes. So, for lesbians on the team, that just left the jealousy à trois, as we called them, three women who had not yet managed to come out even to themselves but were involved in a triangle of jealousy complicated, in my opinion, by a lack of sex. And, of course, there were the four definitely straight women on the team, Susan Thurmond, Amanda Severson, Kathy Jones, and Thalia Peterson. Somehow we were all more and more aware of who was who. Somehow that individual clarity seemed to dissolve our team clarity.

※

One day, near the end of the season, Montgomery came into practice a half hour late. Her face was white and drawn. "Get dressed," she ordered. "Dean Roper is coming to talk with you." And she turned and went into her office.

"Wha—?" we all said to one another, just barely damp and sweaty in our practice jerseys.

When we came out after pulling on sweats, Montgomery told us to wait in the gym. Roper came out with a "Father Knows Best" smile on his face. "Carson," he said, forcing a twinkle to light his eye, "why don't you come on in first."

"What?" Thalia kept saying, her voice pitched high. "I don't get it."

Thalia was not a good actress. It was obvious that she was the only one who *did* get it.

Five minutes later, Carson came out glaring. "It's the Inquisition," she mumbled, throwing herself on a bench.

"Go on and get dressed, Carson," Roper ordered, knowing an agitator when he saw one.

I expected Carson to challenge Roper, at least by hesitating before obeying, but perhaps she realized the safety of the rest of us lay in not exciting him further. Carson left and Roper called in Stella, who strode before the dean like a gazelle leading a turtle.

One by one, Roper called us into Montgomery's office. Except for Carson, each returned to her seat on the bench. No one spoke a word. Finally, second from the last, my turn came. I was surprised to see Coach sitting next to the big oak desk in her own office. I couldn't believe that she had had to sit through each of the interviews. Roper sat at Montgomery's desk. Tension sprang out of his face in beads of sweat. He leaned forward, no longer smiling. "We've had some problems on the team, I understand." He spoke slowly. I could tell that despite his obvious discomfort he was savoring every moment of this scandal. "Many of the women I've spoken to have felt unsafe because of the lesbianism on the team. What about you?"

"I feel safe."

"Are you a lesbian?" Roper looked as if he had tasted the word. I glanced involuntarily at Montgomery, expecting her to protect me. But her eyes were blank. I stared at her folded hands, realizing she had been forced to sit through even the interrogation of Stella. My eyes moved from her hands to her chest. She wasn't breathing. Suddenly I wanted to protect *her*. My head raced, frantically searching for the right response. I thought of Jackie, of Stella and Montgomery. Then, the miracle — I felt myself rising, bobbing up to the surface of the swamp. I faced Roper squarely. I remained utterly silent.

I willed him to accept my refusal to answer, and he did. He said, "We'll get to the bottom of this, young miss. Whichever side you're on, you may be sure it will be straightened out." He added, "So to speak."

When I went back into the gym the whole team looked at me, and I knew they were trying to read my face, to guess what I had said. No one moved, as we waited for Roper to call in the last of us — Thalia Peterson. Roper was not a shrewd man. In fact, after this slip I knew he was downright stupid: He never did call in Thalia; he left by a back door, and Montgomery came and told us to shower and go to dinner.

※

"Okay, no one is leaving the locker room," Kathy Jones said two days later after practice.

"What is this, a holdup?" Carson stood, pants unzipped and one shoe in hand as if she were ready to fight.

"Be mellow, McDuffy," Amanda Severson warned.

Susan Thurmond was suddenly at Amanda's and Kathy's sides. Three of the four straight women stood in a block. Thalia had her back turned and was throwing things in her gym bag as fast as a bank robber would shovel bills. She stood and headed for the door, without having even brushed her hair. Thalia had a nose for danger.

"Where're you going, Peterson?" Kathy said. Since when was Thalia called "Peterson?"

Thalia tossed her blonde hair, ran fingers through the top. "This has nothing to do with me."

"Oh, I think it may have everything to do with you."

A First Lady smile and, "I'm real busy. Gotta go."

"I bet you could spare five minutes," Amanda said, walking toward Thalia. Thalia sat on the bench, a good distance away from the rest of us.

"So what's going on?" Carson struck her most butch stance, facing off with the straight girls.

"Mellow, McDuffy."

"Don't tell me what to be, Severson." Carson stepped forward, slitting her eyes.

"So what's going on?" Jackie finally said, the only sensible tone of voice so far.

"We thought we should all talk," Amanda said. I understood the first "we" to mean the straight women. "Look, we still have a chance to make it to the play-offs. And this ... this bullshit about lesbians on the team, well..."

"Fuck yourself!" Carson screamed. "You all can just go fuck yourselves."

Kathy Jones lunged for Carson. But she stopped half an inch from her face. "Shut up, McDuffy. You ain't got a chip on your shoulder, you got a block of wood so big you can't see your own ugly face in the mirror."

Carson went for the throat. In a split second, Jackie was behind her, wrangling Carson's arms off Kathy. I tried to arrest her kicking legs. At the same time, Amanda subdued Kathy.

"For goodness sakes, *listen!*" Amanda screamed.

We all turned when we heard Thalia say, in a near-growl, "Let me out of here." But Susan Thurmond blocked the door.

What was this? The straight girls getting ready to pound the shit out of us? Threaten or blackmail us? I started to sweat all over again.

With eyes like icicles, Kathy pierced Carson. Not looking away for a second, she said, "Go ahead, Amanda."

"Kathy, Susan, and I wanted to tell you, well, we wanted to talk. None of us three gave any names, okay? None of us told Roper anything. We didn't say whether we were straight or what." Amanda sat on the bench and tears flowed into her eyes. "Geez, we used to be a *team*. We've got to pull together. Look, we *are* pulling together. See, that's why we haven't heard anything more from Roper. Don't you get it? He got no information. *None*."

"You mean none of you said you were straight?" I asked, slow as always, taking it in.

"No. None of us said anything to that sleaze bag. What about the rest of you?"

"I didn't give him a clue."

"Nope."

"I just told him I didn't know and didn't give a shit, either."

"I told him I was a lesbian," Carson said slowly, looking at her feet. "I said I had no idea if anyone else was."

"You take the hard road every time," Kathy Jones almost whispered.

"I just tell the truth." Carson tried to harden, but looked soft for once in her life.

"That's everyone but you, Thalia." We all turned to the end of the bench where Thalia sat, her face hot and red. We watched her muster all the aristocratic poise she could, but it wasn't much. For the first time in the year I'd known her, I saw the woman lose it.

Her hands were shaking, with anger, I thought. Thalia had assumed her power in this situation. The past few days she had been looking more serene, beauteous, as if a struggle had been finally resolved. Never had it occurred to her that she would be sacrificed for the triumph of sisterhood.

"*Thalia,*" pressed Amanda, "what did *you* tell Roper?"

"He didn't call me in."

"Right. Then obviously you had already spoken to him."

Thalia stood and managed to say, "I have no idea what any of you are talking about." Those narrow eyes nearly crossed.

We sat and stared in silence for a moment at her straight posture, her composed and high cheekbones, her long graceful arms. Suddenly I saw a long line of stern, puritan women, severely beautiful and rich women, stacking up behind her as if she were in a house of mirrors. Mothers, grandmothers, and great-grandmothers, all of them echoing, "I have no idea what any of you are talking about ... I have no idea what any of you are talking about ... I have no idea..."

✳

We partied that night. Me, Jackie, Susan, Amanda, Kathy, Carson, even the jealousy à trois. Everyone except for Stella, Coach, and of course Thalia, gathered in Jackie's room and hashed over everything we'd missed this year during Thalia Peterson's reign of terror. We died laughing at every story, rocked in our relief. Safe, we were all safe. For fun, we raked Thalia over the coals, tore her apart hair by hair, gesture by gesture. At first it seemed we took joy in pure and simple hatred. Thalia Peterson was the catheter for the evil venom in our souls. Oh, but we were cruel.

But then we crossed over that magic line into the dark blue waters of early morning. We left Thalia behind like a wrecked ship, useless, history. Slowly and carefully, we began telling stories from last year, the old ones, only now elaborating on the jock, punch-line versions to fill in nuances, shades of meaning, our feelings. Some of us told our coming-out stories and of our fears of others on the team finding out. We all spoke, our voices like tentative fingers, about how much the team meant to us, how each woman was an experience in our lives we could never replace. Outside the one window of Jackie's dorm room, daylight permeated the sky. I switched off the desk lamp we'd had on. Even Carson, sitting slumped on the corner of Jackie's bed, said in her husky voice, "Yeah, I guess I blew it in the locker room. We're all pulling together. Yeah, we're all pulling our share, aren't we?"

"Yeah," I said. I felt as if I finally understood the source of brilliance in a perfectly executed defense, in a flawless three-on-two fast break, in a full-court press, when every team member was exactly where she was supposed to be. I felt as if that brilliance had just been laid in my lap. I understood something new, something as deep as it ever gets.

✳

We did not make it to the play-offs. Carson did not make the Eastern Division All-Star team (though Thalia did). And Jackie and I didn't make it through to the end of the year. She began seeing another woman on the team, finally bringing out one corner of the jealous triangle (which allowed the remaining two to collapse together in yet another torrid basketball romance). Naturally I was devastated, and mushed through my final exams like a rain-soaked puppy, stupid, sloppy, miserable, and eager for the tiniest show of kindness. On the night before my last exam, the phone rang. When I answered, Jackie's voice filled the receiver. I hadn't talked to her in three weeks and was so overwhelmed by her presence in my ear that I didn't even listen to what she said.

"You okay, babe?" she repeated. "I just wanted to say hello."

"I miss you, Jackie," I blurted.

"I know, babe. But we had a good year anyway, didn't we?"

"Yeah," I said, crying, and then sobbing. In spite of everything, it had been the best year of my life.

TO ANNA

ELISSA GOLDBERG

August 26, 1989

Dear Anneleh,

I can't sleep so good these days. Nu, it's old age. Two sleeping pills I already took and nothing works. I get up, I walk around, I lay back down and I'm staring at the ceiling. It's okay. What do I have to do tomorrow that's so important I need a good night's sleep?

Oi, but not sleeping is not the worst of being old, let me tell you. It's just lucky you died before me, may you rest in peace, you didn't have the chance to be so lonely. At least we had each other we could talk to. These days, I'm lucky to be on the porch when the mailman, Milt, comes by. Once in a while I see someone at the Senior Center, we have lunch. But the old gang, I'm the last of them. We put Harry in the ground not three months ago, may he, too, rest in peace.

So who can I tell what I have to tell? Marilyn comes by, yes. She comes in, she straightens the place, she brings some food with her, and then she leaves. Not one minute can she spare to listen to an answer to her own question: How are you? Her own father, she should be so busy. But Anneleh, what I have to tell you she wouldn't understand anyway.

Today I went to a softball game. Usually I go to the courthouse. That you know. But today, it was a Saturday, so I went to a softball game in the park near our house. Not so far to walk, but me, I'm an old man. I'm on a walk, I get tired, I see some people around, I go sit down, and there's a softball game. Nu, no big deal. But these boys I'm watching playing, Anna, these boys, it takes me a whole twenty minutes to see what makes no sense. These boys, they have bosoms. Oi, it makes no sense to me. Here I'm watching what I think are good playing boys, and they're girls the whole time. Yeah, some of them had long hair, but I too lived through the sixties. Hair, it makes no difference. And anyway, Anna, these girls, I'm telling you, if they was wearing dresses you might still think they were boys. Okay, maybe no, but the way they were with each other, the way they caught the balls, the way they stood out in outfield, they looked like boys. How, I can't explain it.

Nu, so I'm sitting there wishing I had someone to turn to with my revelation. I should be so lucky. When I look again and who do I see? I see Mitzi, Marilyn's youngest. Mitzeleh, can you believe it? She's the pitcher. I know what you're thinking. Jack, you say, your eyes are no good, you're an old man, your mind is tired. How do you know Mitzi's playing ball? But, Anna, I see Mitzi, I know Mitzi. She's my own flesh and blood. Okay, you want the truth? I'll tell you the truth. Somebody next to me, another one of these girls I think is a boy, she yells to Mitzi, "Strike 'er out, Mitzi!" And I look, thinking, nu, I know a Mitzi too, and sure enough there pitching ball is our Mitzi. Okay, can you believe it? I see her twice a month on a Friday night and does she ever tell me she plays ball? Unlike her dear mother, she talks to me, but does she ever once tell me what she does on Saturdays? No. I have to go to the park to find out.

And she's a good player, Anna, you would be proud. She throws the ball, she catches the ball. She even hits not so bad, you should see. Then the game is over, and she disappears. At first, I think, I'll wait, but then I'm tired. I think, I'll tell her when I see her what a good ball player she is.

But then something happens that makes me think I won't say nothing to her. On my way out, I see all these other people milling around a certain area. There are tables and chairs all set up, and I see some trophies. So I guess that this game I watched is one in a tournament. Nu, what else could explain so many people around? I'm not so dumb. So I go up to someone and ask her who sponsors this tournament. And she says the LCP. And I say, oh, and who is this LCP, I never heard of such a thing. And she tells me it's the Lesbian Community Project. The Lesbian Community Project, I shake my head. Suddenly I am wore out and I walk home.

So, I think, maybe all these girls are lesbians. Lesbians, Anna, they love other girls. But what I can't understand is why Mitzi plays with them. I think and I think, all evening I think about this. Maybe she's friends with some of them. Maybe she couldn't get on no other ball team. Maybe they asked her to join their team.

But, Anna, when I get in bed and close my eyes, it becomes clear to me. Our Mitzi, she's a lesbian. That's why she plays on their team. Nu, she too looked like a boy to me at first, I didn't recognize her. And does she ever once mention a boy she's interested in? No. Her sisters tell me about their boyfriends. Franny's even getting married next month, you would be proud. But with Mitzeleh, we don't talk about such things. And she's a big kid now, old enough to start a family.

So then I'm staring at the ceiling. I'm trying to sleep, but who can sleep with such a mindful? Oi, I'm thinking, she'll be so lonely. She'll be all alone as an old woman without any kinder. I know such women who never married. They talk too much. They can't help themselves, they're so lonely. Our Mitzi, she'll never marry, she'll never have any children, she'll never see her son's bris or her daughter's wedding. And what will the relatives think? Maybe they should be wandering by some ball game too. Nu, what do I say to them? "Don't worry, she's not one of them." But she is.

So I turn over on my side. But I can't sleep. I get up, I make myself a little warm milk, maybe a piece of toast. I sit down and start writing you this letter. I write until this last paragraph. Then I feel tired, I go to the couch to rest a little. But just as I'm falling asleep, I remember something. And this I have not remembered for over seventy years. Nu, don't turn in your grave I didn't tell you this before. I didn't tell myself either.

When I was six we came to America. My brother was eight, it was 1910. My father had been killed three years before by the Poles in a raid on our village. My mother was now taking us to the Land of Freedom, with two suitcases, a babushka on her head, and her friend, Rubina. Rubina was a large woman with red frizzy hair. She was not married. She had been a neighbor of ours, but when my father died she came to live with us. She and my mother, they were our parents.

When things became too hard to stay any longer in Poland, we packed our things to go. But Rubina, she couldn't get papers for leaving. She had no relatives in America. So we decided she should take the identity of my father, may he rest in peace. My mother cut Rubina's hair and dressed her in my father's clothes. I remember looking up and not recognizing this stranger, even though I understood our plans. We were to call her Papa, and she would go by my father's name.

We lived a far ways from the Atlantic. It took us several days to travel by foot and then a train to the shore. Then we had to wait a few weeks for passage. During this time, Rubina caught a cold. Not a bad one at first, but her cough, I remember, it kept her awake at night. When we were on the ship, huddled together below deck, crowded into the cattle area, her cough became worse. We could not make tea. We could not keep her warm enough. My mother, she wrapped Rubina up in her featherbed, but Rubina continued to shiver and cough. Always coughing. For three weeks, she was coughing.

The worst part was that the more sick Rubina became, the more she looked like a woman. Her eyes were larger, and her cheekbones, they grew sharp and pronounced. And when she coughed, she did not sound like a man who has a deep voice. The people around us, the same Jews who were traveling with us below deck for all this time, they began to talk. They began to wonder.

We did not know of their suspicions until we arrived at Ellis Island. Oi, and then, such a shandela, a shame, I can barely mention it here. Of course, when Rubina walked from the ship, she looked like a ghost. And the authorities, they recognized this. They were always on the lookout for sick people who they would not admit to their country. But on top of this, our ship neighbors, people we had shared our bread with, they told the authorities of their suspicions. This is not a man, they said. This is a woman, and she has been living as a husband to this woman, and they pointed to my mother.

Anna, I have not thought of this in all this time. I shake as I write of this. The authorities, they pushed Rubina into a side room and whatever they did to her, they found she was not a man. When she walked from that room, she was

99

crying. She was bruised and her clothes, my father's clothes that hung limp on her already from being so ill, they were torn. And she did not walk from this room alone. They pushed her out and called her names, names I could not understand, names I can no longer remember. And they led her back to the ship. They were sending her back. They would not let my mother and Rubina say good-bye. They would not let them talk. And the whole time, the people watching this, they were cheering the authorities on. They were applauding these monsters.

Watching this, Anna, I was a little boy. I wanted to run to her, to scream and pull her back to us, to my mother. But the whole time this was happening, the whole time they pushed her from the side room to the boat, my mother and brother and I, we did not move. It was as if this strange force was cast around us, a fence. Now I know that if we had screamed or shouted our horror, we would have all been sent back. Back then, I only felt paralyzed.

We never heard from Rubina again. I know my mother tried to send letters, but she got no response. Where did she send them? I don't know. But her sadness she carried with her to her grave.

Anneleh, I'm an old man. What do I know of such things? Maybe Rubina and my mother, maybe they were just friends, neighbors who helped each other through the hard times. But then again, they loved each other. For a time we were a family. Nu, maybe my mother, maybe she too liked the girls. Maybe if she had grown up in the United States of America, in Mitzi's time, maybe she would also play softball.

I have sat here a long time already writing to you. The sky is now getting pink outside. Soon the birds will wake up and I will feed them. What I will feed them I don't know. But I will feed them.

I think, Anna, about those people at Ellis Island, the other Jews who crossed the ocean with us. What they did to my mother's life, what they did to Rubina's life, they will never know. They were scared. Nu, the Jews were scapegoats to the Nazis and to the Poles. My mother and Rubina, they were scapegoats to these Jews. And Mitzi, her difference is so bad I should kill her or send her back to Poland? No. Better she should play softball.

This staying up all night, I find out many things. If I weren't an old man already, maybe I would do it more often. But Anna, my bones are tired now. Maybe I'll go lay down for a while. The birds can wait.

Until we meet again,
Jack

A DATE
WITH DETH

KAREN BARBER

A llie was not certain of the exact moment when she decided to ignore her friends' warnings and go out with Deth. But then, looking at the big picture, it doesn't really matter. You could even say that if Allie was looking at the big picture at all, she probably never would have gone out with Deth. But, she did. And really, that's all that matters now.

Allie's friends had tried — and succeeded — to prevent Allie from seeing Deth in the past. They'd said that she wouldn't be good for her, that Allie didn't need that kind of trouble. She had enough to contend with. God, when was that? Probably not long after Elizabeth left for that sleazy guy who lived downstairs. Not a pretty scene, you can imagine, but Allie seemed to survive it with more than an ounce of dignity still intact. It was then, after many fits of anger and many hours of crying, that Allie had considered finally meeting Deth and seeing what caused so many women —

and men, for that matter — to be swept away by her mystique.

No one knew much about Deth. Her name, of course, wasn't really Deth. That much, people did know. Her real name was Meredeth, spelled with an "e." How convenient. She was striking-looking; with that, no one could argue. But she wasn't a conventional beauty. You couldn't imagine her on the cover of *Cosmopolitan;* but, if you gave it any thought (and most people did), you could picture her working the runways for high-fashion designers in, say, Paris or Rome. She always dressed in black. Always. But not butch 501s, t-shirt or turtleneck, cowboy boots black. Oh no, not Deth. Deth wore silk blouses, slightly oversized, that elegantly draped her perfectly round breasts. She wore tailored slacks — Dietrich style — and designer shoes. Sometimes she would also wear an evening jacket, also black, that gave her a sophisticated European look. Her hair could only be described as midnight black. She always wore it slicked back, her blunt cut ending about an inch and a half from her shoulders. Her skin was olive, giving some people reason to assume she was of Mediterranean origin. No one ever asked her.

No one ever saw Deth during the day. She appeared only at night, at trendy — and not so trendy — lesbian bars around town. Most, if not all, of her acquaintances couldn't even imagine Deth enjoying a walk in the park with a puppy or playing tag with children on the beach. Her natural environment was in those bars where lonely women drink away their sorrows and where misery loves company.

Deth never entered a bar with a woman. But ninety-nine percent of the time, she would leave with one. Attractive dykes, unattractive dykes, old dykes, young dykes, it didn't really seem to matter to Deth. When leaving the club, Deth always looked as if she had found the woman of her dreams. Her pickups, on the other hand, though never forced to leave with Deth, always — always — seemed a bit apprehensive. It was strange. Here they were leaving with one of the most attractive women to ever have graced the room with her presence — a woman *they* had made moves on — and yet they weren't really sure if they should be doing it or not. It wasn't an obvious thing, their eyes weren't yelling "Help" or anything, but if you studied them, from the time that Deth answered their call through the time they walked out the door, you could sense that the other woman had, well, her doubts about her own judgment. Maybe it was the way their eyes shifted nervously back and forth. Maybe it was how they would unconsciously play with the hem of their shirts, or how they would constantly run their fingers through their hair. Any of these things could have alerted you to their apprehension. But really, it wasn't something a spectator could put a finger on.

That first time, after Elizabeth, Allie's defenses were down. She was depressed. She missed work, she drank. She constantly watched old movies where the heroine died at the end. She listened to Billie Holiday records, scratches and all. And when she wasn't home watching movies or listening to old records, she was out cruising bars, picking up women to prove that women (damn that Elizabeth!) still found her attractive. Her friends began to worry. As well they should have. It was a very ugly thing to have to watch.

Allie saw Deth, that first time, about two weeks after Elizabeth had left her. She imagined that Deth was always around the bars before, but Allie just never noticed. She was, after all, in love with Elizabeth, and had been for three years now. Allie didn't think it strange — being terribly in love and all — not to have noticed this strikingly good-looking woman before. She had been devoted to Elizabeth, as only a good monogamous dyke lover could be. But now, with Elizabeth having gone off to fuck that man, things were different. She wanted Deth. She craved her company. Being with Deth was something that Allie had to do.

But Allie's friends, bless their concerned hearts, intervened. She's trouble, Allie, just open your eyes. What do you know about her, Allie? You know nothing about her, that's what. She's never with the same woman twice, Allie, is that what you want to mess with? You don't need more heartache, babe, you need stability. We'd tell you to ask someone who knows, someone Deth's been with, but no one's around. They just don't seem to come back, or at least they wait a while before they do, and by then we don't remember who they were. Is that a good sign, Allie? Just forget her. Please.

Maybe they had a point, Allie thought. Maybe what she needed now wasn't something Deth could give her. Maybe she needed something else, something more. But what?

Rachel. Yep, Rachel was that evasive "what" that Allie needed. Allie had met her in the video store while returning Greta Garbo in *Camille*. Rachel was renting *Love Story*. It was fate.

They shared much of the same tastes in the arts. They liked the same restaurants. They wore the same type of clothes. They liked the same kind of sex. Obviously, something so good wouldn't last. But for the time being, Allie's friends were relieved. Those she hadn't alienated with her drunken after-Elizabeth antics were able to rest easy, knowing that, for now, Allie was emotionally secure. As a matter of fact, Allie seemed to be her old self again. She rarely drank, she rarely went out. She and Rachel usually stayed home, made dinner for friends, went to bed early. For a good six months they appeared to be happy.

But wouldn't you know it, Allie's luck was about to run out. Rachel, it seems, was more like Elizabeth than Allie cared to imagine. Allie knew that Rachel and Elizabeth shared some important personality traits; that was, truth be told, what really attracted Allie to Rachel in the first place. But what Allie didn't know was that Rachel shared Elizabeth's taste for men. That is, she didn't know until she got off work early one day and bopped on over to Rachel's hoping to surprise her. Surprise, although certainly the *right* word, was most definitely an understatement. When she opened the door (with a key she had taken the liberty to have made for herself — she knew Rachel wouldn't mind) and saw Rachel screwing some hairy man right there on the living room floor (a man that looked suspiciously like a neighbor of Rachel's), something snapped in Allie. Something big. She marched out, slamming the door behind her.

Having lost her last two lovers to men, Allie wasn't in the highest of spirits. She was, once again, downright depressed. Not only that, she hated her dead-end job, she hated her apartment (complete with roaches and two noisy kids downstairs), she hated the fact that she couldn't walk down the city's streets without an incredible fear (paranoia?) that she was going to be a victim of some sort of random violence, and she hated her sister for calling to tell her that she wasn't going to be able to come visit after all, that something suddenly came up. Simply put, you could say that Allie *hated,* period.

Much like before, Allie began to drink. She began to stay up late to catch black-and-white tear-jerkers on TV. She dusted off her old Barry Manilow records. But *unlike* before, Allie's friends were more detached. It was nothing intentional, but they all seemed to be wrapped up in their own lives. Susan had just started an important new job that was taking up a lot of her time. Alice recently found a new girlfriend after years of looking. Kyle's mother just died of cancer. Kathy found God. Denise just wasn't in the mood to deal with another round of Allie's bitter depression. And who could blame her?

Allie's friends' lack of concern only added to Allie's self-doubt and self-hatred. Allie had reached the end of her rope — albeit a short one (she was never all *that* stable) — and decided that maybe a walk on the wild side was what would be best for her. No one was there to give her advice; she was in this alone now, calling her own shots. What did she have to lose? She was lonely, depressed, and her therapist was out of town. So, Allie made a decision that Friday night. She decided to look for Deth.

When she arrived at the club, it was already smoky, although she was only one of a handful of women out before eleven o'clock. She seated herself at the bar and proceeded to down three gin and tonics in what seemed like record time, even to herself. She smiled. She liked surprising herself. When you're depressed — really, really, depressed — little things mean a lot.

Shortly after midnight, Deth made an appearance. With her left hand she removed her sunglasses, revealing eyes that were dark, dark brown, almost black. Her right hand held a burning cigarette, unfiltered — Deth didn't kid herself. A few heads turned when Deth walked in. However, the women who were talking and laughing with each other didn't really seem to notice her. But Allie did. Whether from the alcohol or her state of mind, Allie decided that now was not the time for coy pickup games that would take a lot of time to play themselves out. She wanted Deth, wanted her bad, and she wasn't going to waste any time getting her. But she couldn't be overzealous; Deth wasn't someone you pressured into anything.

She decided, instead, to sit back and stare at Deth. Just stare, and *will* Deth over to her side of the bar. Deth, looking as breathtaking as ever, made her way through the now-crowded bar to the dance floor. Allie noticed that Deth had a preference for the more progressive sounds of "mope rock" bands, with their dark, foreboding, and cluttered guitar sounds. The more morbid, the better, it seemed. Deth never danced with anyone. Instead, she slowly and without effort swayed to the music, eyes closed, a slight smirk on her lips. Was she aware of how good she looked out there, or was she really just totally involved with whatever she heard in her own head? Allie wasn't sure.

The song ended and Deth, waking from her dance stupor, walked off the dance floor in Allie's direction. Allie involuntarily took a gasp of air and shivered as a chill swept through her body. Deth met Allie's stare, which by now had lost some of its original boldness, and held it. Was Allie losing her nerve? Maybe, but she would stand her ground. She'd show her friends, once and for all, how she could take control of her life when need be.

If you were watching Allie and Deth's exchange from afar, chances are you'd be intrigued. There was something so very sexy and seductive about the way Deth moved and worked her willing prey. She was so totally at ease with herself, with her beauty and powers, that if you were in her clutches you stood very little chance of ever freeing yourself. And for a fleeting moment, every woman who had ever been wrapped up with Deth had tried to break that spell. Some more than others, to be sure, but each one did try. But Deth would smile, run the smooth back of her hand along your love-starved face, and that would be that. Whatever suffering compelled you to search out Deth in the first place took over your senses. You became hers. Most women whimpered and collapsed into Deth's arms. She'd gently hold them, rock them back and forth, and whisper seductively in their ear.

Allie was no different. Like everyone before her, she glanced hopefully around the familiar bar, wishing a friend (hadn't she seen Susan come in a while ago?) would run over to her and drag her away from this dark and mysterious woman. But when no one did — when no one cared enough to help — Deth and her charms became all the more powerful. Deth had won and Allie would get only what she had wanted.

When Allie, clinging to the tall stranger, ascended the steep stairs leading to the street, she looked back only once. She wondered if she should have told someone, Susan maybe, that she was leaving with Deth. But then she realized how foolish she was being. After all, in the end, everyone knows when you've had a date with Deth.

DADDY'S HOME

JESSIE LYNDA LASNOVER

I was sitting on the floor scrubbing the cracks between the bricks of the wall when she asked me the question. She was a big strong girl, with short, curly dark hair and rather sad-looking, very dark brown eyes. She didn't look mean. She was on the floor as I was, scrubbing cracks in the wall a few feet to my right. I thought maybe she was Italian, or Greek, or maybe even Armenian. The sad quality of her heavy-lidded eyes was really sexy. When she caught me watching her, she smiled. The hairs along the back of my neck stood up. I forced my eyes away from her and looked at the wall.

"Are you gay?" she asked.

Just as I always had, in all the other places, I said, "No." It was always the first question the other girls asked. It made my belly tense up, and I felt as if I was under attack. Years of living with the necessity of keeping my thoughts secret made lying second nature. I felt the prickly feel of her gaze on me while I stared at the wall and kept on scrubbing.

My fingers were starting to lock; I was double-jointed, and the scrubbing was making them lock into the wrong angle, the joints pressing hard against the inside skin of my fingers. Fucking cracks, I thought — fucking woman that gave us this job cleaning already-spotless cracks. I hated the woman, I could hear her gossiping and laughing in the other room with the rest of the staff. She had red hair and a lazy southern accent. She liked to joke around and try to make us like her with her easy southern friendliness; but she was a hard woman and she carried the keys. She didn't like to see a girl sitting quietly, lost in the contentment of reading a book. She thought we were all too stupid to read a book and we should be talking, kidding back, playing the game, or working.

It was funny, but most of the staff had red hair, even the snotty Mexican one who treated us as if we were too filthy to touch. "Babies," she'd call us, and say, "If you were the big girls you pretend to be, you'd know how to behave and wouldn't be here." And the old one, the head lady, also called us babies; but she said we were *her* babies, as though that would bring trust. There was one with long brown hair who looked like a kid; she didn't have any power. She was nice, she sympathized; she didn't know anything about living. Some of the meanest girls gave her a hard time. They said, "She ain't nobody, she can't tell me what to do — fuck her." She cried, sometimes. Eventually she started working the late-night shift, when we were all asleep.

That first day at the California Youth Authority School for Girls, I wanted to read a book. I wanted to be alone in my room. I wanted this girl to mind her own fucking business and leave me alone, to get her sad eyes off of me. I glanced out of the corner of my eye at her and I saw she was smiling, watching me and smiling. I turned and glared at her. "Anything else you want to know?" I demanded.

111

"No," she said, still smiling at me, "I just like to look at you. I think you're cute and I'd sure like to squeeze your body ... I think you'd like it too."

I felt my face flush red and I hated it for giving away my feelings. I let my hair fall to cover my face as I bent toward the wall and scrubbed, and I thanked God, if there was one, for my long hair. I felt her watching me. Her eyes sent heat to my body. The side of me facing her burned. I was sure she realized just what she was doing to me, but I kept silent and waited for her to stop, to leave me alone. After a while she did.

After lunch we went over to the school and got our classes assigned. Sad Eyes wasn't in any of my classes. From now on I'd be able to go to school and wouldn't, I hoped, have to scrub any more fucking cracks. I fit into the routine of the place, like I always did, kept quiet, read when I could, and watched the politics of the unit.

I hated Fridays — we had group therapy. All fifty of the girls on the unit sat in a circle along with the staff, the two teachers assigned to our unit for groups, our unit psychologists (we had two), and any guests the facility invited. Therapy lasted a couple of hours and was torture. On the better Fridays one of the psychologists would lecture. One lecture was even about LSD; the psychologist had been in an experimental drug project, and he told us how drugs rot your brain. He wasn't too bright. A couple of the black girls played a game on him, and he spent the whole time telling them what LSD felt like — he never noticed the sly grins they were giving the rest of us.

Other times, we had to discuss any girl caught breaking a rule. We each took a turn giving our opinion, while she sat in the middle with all our eyes on her. Sometimes the girl in the center would cry. Girls coming up for parole said all kinds of phony, "correct" things, putting the girl down for breaking a rule. Usually it was for smoking in

112

her room. We all did that. I did it every night; I never got caught.

The youngest girl on the unit got caught several times. Her name was Jackie. She was fifteen. "Jackie," they'd say, "Why do you do it? Why do you keep breaking the rules? Don't you want to get out of here?"

Then she'd cry. It made me sick. All the girls in turn would ask, "Why do you do it? You shouldn't do that, Jackie; you know better." But they all did it too and the fucking staff knew it and would smile so approvingly as each girl in turn became a hypocrite. The staff was breaking our loyalty, our family feeling; they thought it was unhealthy to be loyal to each other. Not one girl said, "Why did you get *caught,* Jackie?"

When my turn came I said, "No comment." My parole was denied five times, the maximum allowed for a girl on the regular program, because I always said, "No comment." They said I refused to participate in the program.

I was there because I kept running away from home. I was a "chronic runaway." I ran away because my parents were crazy. My home was unpredictable; everyone was on drugs, and I couldn't learn the way to act to avoid getting beaten — the rules changed all the time. It was safer being locked up. But I hated the games, and I just would not play. The one time they put me in the middle, I refused to say anything at all.

Sad Eyes's name was Bobbi. She was a real butch. Because she was underage, she was picked up for being gay and hanging out with other gay people. They thought she could be cured by locking her up in an all-girl institution where the majority of the girls acted gay — it was the thing to do, though most reverted to boys when released. They told Bobbi she had to wear lipstick and dresses to get out. She held out for a long time; she was there almost as long as I was. I watched Bobbi. I didn't ever become her friend, but I was interested in her story.

In our unit, there were three or four "families," with parents, kids, cousins, aunts and uncles, and even grandparents. I usually stayed out of the families; I liked to be on my own — I was a solitary.

Bobbi set up her family over on the west side of the dayroom. Her family was pretty small, just parents and kids. Bobbi was the daddy. Her wife was named Liz. I knew Liz from outside. She was a straight girl. She'd been in a foster home of some blood relatives of mine. Of course she was doomed — my real family was crazy. Liz had very white skin and blonde hair. She was kind of innocent, and she liked to be in with the in crowd, which was why she joined the family. Their kids were three very tough black girls, all real butches with lovers on other units. Sometimes they carried on temporary love affairs with girls on the unit who then usually got attacked at school and beaten up by the lovers. I'd seen this game in most of the places I'd been in, and found it pretty boring.

But Liz and Bobbi were different; what started out a game turned into something real. Bobbi was a real butch — and nobody can make love like a real butch. A butch plays a role: She is a tender woman with the skill that comes from being a woman and knowing all the secrets of a woman's body, yet she is as masterful and controlling as a man — real sexy. Liz fell in love with Bobbi. I don't know what Bobbi felt — she was tough. But Liz let it show all over her. She radiated love at Bobbi. Her face glowed; her smile was special. She touched Bobbi's arm with her arm when they passed; she moved her body close to Bobbi when they sat. Liz hung on Bobbi's every word and brought her gifts, gave her the dessert off her tray, saved her the best seat at a movie or the first use of the washer. "This is for Bobbi," she'd say. And Bobbi would smile and say, "Thanks, baby." Liz was in a state of bliss.

I watched them. I saw how Liz looked. I wondered what Bobbi did to make Liz look like that. Once I sat next to them

114

in the movie, and when the lights went down I heard Bobbi say, "Come closer, baby." I heard rustling and a low groan from Liz. The heat from them burned into my thighs. Another time, I walked in the laundry room and they were on the floor next to the dryer. Liz didn't see me. Her face was flushed; she had her eyes closed; she was moaning. Bobbi looked right into my eyes and smiled as a lion or a stallion might smile. "That's good, baby," she said. I stumbled out of the room.

I decided to stay away from them for a while. I tried not to watch them, and I kept myself on the other side of the dayroom. Sometimes I'd look up and Bobbi would look at me and smile. I'd look away.

I started talking to a group of girls. I made some friends. I joined a big family and got entangled in relationships with sisters and cousins. We got reprimanded because our family got so big it became a threat to the staff. "You don't need a family," the old redhead said. "You're all my babies."

Sitting in the dayroom with my back to the door, I felt whenever Bobbi came into the room. The hairs on the back of my neck would stand up and then I'd smell her behind me. I'd take in a deep breath. I'd feel dizzy.

Early one morning, she gave me her bathrobe. She brought it to my room, opened the door, and threw it on my bed. "Don't wear it out of your room," she said, smiling at me. I felt my face flush hot as she laughed and walked away. The feeling of her filled up my whole room with heat, and I felt like I couldn't breathe.

My neighbor, Pat, talked to me through the crack where the walls met at the end away from the door. "What happened?" she said. "Why did Bobbi come to your room?"

"Nothing," I said. "I left my book in the dayroom, and she brought it to me. Do you have a match?" She passed me a match and we had a cigarette together, blowing the smoke out the window between the bars. I sang songs every night to Pat. She couldn't sleep, so I sang, "Lemon tree, very pretty, and the lemon flower is sweet, but the fruit of the poor lemon is impossible to eat...," and she slept.

Each of us lived in a single room. It had a steel cot with a thin mattress, a wool blanket, a lumpy little pillow, and cotton sheets; a steel desk and chair; a closet with built-in drawers; a toilet and a sink. Every part of the room was visible to anyone looking in the window that was set in the door, even the toilet — there was no privacy. Opposite the door a barred window looked out on the grounds, where grass led to a wall with barbed wire. Low buildings with barred windows like ours dotted the grass, and at one end there was a tower with big windows that had a lady inside watching everyone who walked outside the buildings. Nobody ever escaped.

Many times I thought about becoming a mouse. I would run under the door and down the hall, past all the other girls' rooms, and out to the main door. Under that and outside, in the sun ... I'd run, in my fantasy, across the grass toward the wall. I never made it out. Sometimes a big cat would come and kill me; sometimes I got squashed under someone's shoe or under a cart carrying our food or linens. Once I got to the wall, but could find no way out under the brick, no crack anywhere I could crawl under. So I always had to come back to my room and become me again.

The robe smelled like Bobbi, so I never washed it. I slept with it every night — my secret lover — breathing the smell of Bobbi deep into my soul. Once I felt her and looked up; she was framed in the window of my door, smiling at me. She knows, I thought, but she won't tell; I am still safe.

I had a needle in my room I'd been using to sew buttons on a blouse. I heated it with a match and opened my blouse. I picked up a bottle of liquid eyeliner from my desk and opened it. I settled back on my bed and put the eyeliner on the ledge of my steel headboard. I dipped the needle in the eyeliner and then pierced my left breast, above my heart. I tattooed a dot, then another dot, and another. It hurt, but it was a sweet pain — all my love was in that pain. I spelled out "Bobbi" with the dots on my breast; my secret and the keeper of my secret.

That evening, after showers, as I walked to my room I kept going and went to Pat's room. The staff woman at the end of the hall watched me, but from that distance I knew she couldn't tell if I was entering my own room or not. Pat was surprised, but she didn't object when I kissed her and pulled her to the bed. I made love to her every evening after showers until she was paroled. It helped me a little bit, and Pat liked it a lot, though we didn't really love each other. I felt very smug; my reputation had finally paid off. I was never suspected and so was not watched by the staff. I felt like a bank teller who gets away with a million dollars after years of faithful service. I felt as if I was even with Bobbi for trying to blow my cover. I could look at Bobbi and not blush.

Bobbi started wearing dresses and lipstick and using hairspray. She still walked tough; dresses looked silly on her. Liz looked scared. She had a long way to go before parole; a joyride had put a felony on her record: grand theft auto. But Bobbi wanted out. She was granted her parole two months after she started wearing dresses. Liz showed her grief, tears on her face several times every day. My heart turned to ice from trying to keep it hard.

I was alone in the laundry room ironing a shirt the night before Bobbi was supposed to leave. Bobbi came in the room and stood behind me. She kissed the back of my neck. My stomach heaved, wringing my liver and squashing my spleen, my heart stopped, and my throat closed up. I kept my face a mask. "Why did you fuck Pat, bitch?" she whispered in my ear. I wanted to kiss her; my body ached, and my heart felt as if it would slam right through the wall of my chest, but I played my game to the end. I smiled at her and said, "Because I wanted to." She laughed and walked away. "You're so damn good," she said.

There was a good-bye party for Bobbi in the dayroom. We had ice cream and a talent show; girls sang songs and danced. Liz cried. Then Bobbi stood up to say good-bye to us all. She looked at Liz and said, "Baby, this is for you."

Bobbi sang her good-bye song, a real oldie from the forties or fifties — to a slow, lazy beat. She sang, "Daddy's Home." Liz sobbed all through the song. Two of her family kids sat one on each side of her, holding her and watching Bobbi sing. The third kid was putting the make on a new girl in the corner across from me.

The girl next to me said, "Did you know Bobbi has somebody waiting for her on the outside? She turned Liz loose — told her not to look her up when she gets out." The girl on my other side laughed and said, "Hey, that's life. This was just a little jailhouse romance, know what I mean?" We watched Liz cry. Bobbi sang. "Daddy's home, to stay..."

Looking at Liz I thought, that could have been me, if ... if ... I wouldn't let myself think of what.

Bobbi left before we got up the next morning. I was released a month later as "a failure of the program," but I fooled them. I made it. I had learned to play the right game.

SAYING GOOD-BYE

KAREN DALE WOLMAN

It would have been easier if there'd been a funeral. How are you supposed to mourn your best friend if you're not even sure she's dead? They say, "I regret to inform you...," but how do you know? How do you really know?

By the time they told me Taneesha was dead, her family had already flown her body back to Chicago. They had her cremated. There was no service. I guess it doesn't really matter. The Taneesha I knew belonged in Los Angeles. *It just would have been nice to say good-bye.*

Taneesha was the first friend I made in L.A. I met her on the street. I don't mean it the way it sounds. It wasn't sleazy or anything. I was walking east on Hollywood Boulevard one day. Taneesha was walking west. She smiled at me. I smiled back.

You have to live in L.A. to understand how unusual that is. I know people say New York is an unfriendly place, but they don't know L.A. In New York, people don't look at you at all. They just walk by without seeing you. But in L.A., they look at you like you don't exist. They see you, but you're nothing.

That's why it meant so much when Taneesha smiled at me. Most people think you are either crazy or trying to pick them up when you smile. That's why they won't look you in the eye in New York. But Taneesha was just being friendly. I could tell by her eyes.

Taneesha had the kind of eyes that lit up when she talked. They didn't just sparkle, they blazed — bright, hazel, full of laughter. They were so warm, so full of life, you wanted to spill all your secrets. It wasn't a matter of trust. You knew she could read you and you wanted to confirm her intuition.

My eyes are hazel too, but different than Taneesha's. Where hers were bright and shining, mine are dull. Like my hair. It's almost blonde, but not quite. Taneesha's hair was definitive: black, cut short, blunt. People noticed Taneesha.

So there I was, walking down Hollywood Boulevard, looking in store windows, yearning for things I couldn't afford to buy. There was this black leather jacket I'd been visiting every day for a week. I was on my way to see it again when Taneesha smiled at me.

She didn't say hello. She just smiled and asked where I was going. I told her about the jacket and she said she'd come with me. We walked down the boulevard and I told her how I'd look in the jacket. I threw my head back and stood tall. I would be confident if I had the jacket.

Taneesha was already confident. I guess she had to be. She was an actress. She told me all about her career, about the five plays she'd been in. Equity waiver, but still, she had performed. I had never heard of any of the plays, but what did I know about theater? I was just an unemployed woman with a lot of dying dreams and a college degree that didn't seem to mean anything.

I didn't think about death much back then. At twenty-three, death is something that happens to strangers and grandparents. You read about it over coffee and say, "How awful," but it doesn't affect you. You forget about it before breakfast is over. Even when it happens to someone you know, the person is old, always old. You go to a funeral, say how peaceful he looks, and mutter a few prayers. The dirt thuds on the coffin and it's final. Good-bye. *You get to say good-bye.*

Walking up Hollywood Boulevard that day, I told Taneesha all about the jacket. Running my hands over my hips, I showed her how it would fit, snug against my body. I put my hands where the pockets would be, imagining the feel of the leather, supple and strong, smooth and warm. I pulled the collar up high. Feeling the grain rub against my skin, I inhaled the musk. Taneesha entered my fantasy and inhaled with me. As we got close to the store, close to the jacket, I slowed down. The approach wasn't to be taken lightly. Taneesha didn't say anything, but she slowed down too. She understood.

The store window looked just as I remembered it. The jacket was way off in the corner of the display, but my eyes went straight to it. Taneesha saw it too. I didn't have to tell her where to look.

The jacket had sharp, clean lines and braiding across the shoulders. The buckle was steel and polished, the black deep and rich. Strength radiated through the window, making something hunger deep inside of me.

Taneesha did something then that almost ruined our new friendship. As my fantasies were exploring the jacket, Taneesha grabbed my arm and pulled me into the store. I didn't want to go. I knew that I could never afford the jacket. It was better to admire it from a distance.

"That jacket in the window," Taneesha said to the man in the store, "take it out. My friend wants to try it on."

"No, Taneesha, please. It will ruin everything. Let's just go." I was tugging at her arm. She was ignoring me.

"It looks like her size. Take it out of the window," she repeated.

I continued to protest, but the man ignored me, too. I think he was afraid to defy Taneesha. He took the jacket out of the window and held it out to her.

"It's not for me. I told you. It's for her." She glared at the man until he held the jacket in front of me. I was scared, but I had no choice. I tried it on.

As soon as I felt the leather against my skin I was transformed. The jacket wasn't lined; I could feel the roughness against my skin. I pulled the collar up just as I had in my fantasy. I zipped it up halfway and pulled it above my hips. I felt great! I strutted across the store. I couldn't believe I was actually wearing the jacket. We really belonged together. I flipped my hair back over one shoulder. But then I remembered — I didn't have the money. That's why I never tried it on before. How could I give it up once I had a taste of it? Hiding my tears, I took the jacket off and handed it back to the man.

"Wait a minute," Taneesha said. "How much does the jacket cost?"

"Four hundred dollars," the man said. I already knew that. It was more than I'd ever have.

"Can we leave a deposit?"

"Taneesha, I'll never get enough money to pay for it. I can't afford it."

Taneesha ignored me. "If we put some money down, will you hold it for us?"

"Only for a week," he said to her. "You have to put more money down each week or it goes back on sale."

Taneesha turned to me. "How much money do you have?"

"Taneesha. I'll never get four hundred dollars."

"How much money do you have?" she demanded.

Even then, I knew Taneesha ignored what she didn't want to know. I should have remembered that, especially when she told me that the doctors were wrong, that she wasn't going to die. But I wanted to believe she'd live. *Just like I wanted the jacket.*

"Ten dollars." I held out the bill. "And some change, but I need that for the bus."

Taneesha dug a crumpled five out of her pocket. She took the folded ten from my hand and gave both bills to the man. "Give us a receipt. We'll be back next week."

I didn't say anything until we got out of the store. "Taneesha, I'll never get the rest of the four hundred dollars. And I'll never be able to pay you back. Why did you do that? Now we'll lose the whole fifteen dollars."

Taneesha let me finish my little tirade When she spoke, she was calm. She was so logical, it was impossible to argue with her.

"If you think about it too much, it will never happen. If we just go back every week and give him some money, he'll hold the jacket for you. Don't think about the whole four hundred. We'll just come to the store every Saturday and give him whatever money we have. That way, he won't give your jacket to somebody else."

What could I say? The thought of somebody else wearing my jacket made me want to kill.

✳

Taneesha was right. Every Saturday we went back to the store and gave the man some money. One week we only gave him three dollars. But another time we managed to scrape together almost twenty. It didn't matter how much of the money came from me and how much came from Taneesha. I never asked her why she was helping me buy the jacket and she never kept a record of how much she contributed.

We did it for over four months. Every Saturday we went to the store and every Saturday I tried on the jacket. After a few weeks I stopped protesting. I felt like the jacket belonged to me. I have Taneesha to thank for that.

Some Saturdays, when the weather was nice and neither one of us had other plans, we would explore the city. Taneesha had lived in L.A. longer than I had, so she usually came up with the ideas. She knew all sorts of secret places. She showed me an L.A. I didn't know existed, away from the natives and the tourists.

The best place she showed me was a secluded little beach thirty miles up the coast. There were caves filled with puddles from the high tide and pools of water with baby sand crabs. We'd spend the whole day staring at the sea animals and trying to identify the different kinds of seaweed.

Once, on a Wednesday, she took me hiking. Being a weekday, there were no other people around, so we had the woods all to ourselves. When we got to the top of the mountain, Taneesha turned me around and showed me the city. It was one of those clear, smogless days and we could see all of L.A. She pointed south and showed me Catalina Island. At least, she said it was Catalina. I had never been there.

Those are the things I would remember about Taneesha. She was always taking me places, showing me things. I loved seeing them through her eyes. But I knew she wouldn't be around forever. Taneesha was the type of person who would go to Tibet and send me a postcard months later, with no explanation, just a description of the mountains. Or maybe she would call me up and say she was going to New York. I wouldn't hear from her for years, but one day I'd be watching the Tony Awards on TV and Taneesha would appear on stage when they announced Best Actress. I'd phone the hotel and the call would go right through.

124

But I had a part of her as long as she remained in L.A. I expected her to go away. *I thought I'd get to say good-bye.*

One of our favorite things was to sit in Taneesha's living room, drinking hot chocolate and talking for hours, sometimes until the sun rose high over Hollywood. We'd talk hopes and dreams and plans until we were so full the liquid swished around in our stomachs.

I told Taneesha everything: where I went, what I thought, what I said. I knew she had other friends, other dreams, but I liked her mystery. *I figured she told me the important stuff, so the rest didn't matter.*

Early one dawn after hours of chocolate and hours of words, she went into the bathroom. I saw a recent playbill lying in a corner and picked it up. I recognized the name of a small Hollywood theater, but laughed at the title. "Junk Dog Cross"? I opened the playbill, hoping for a synopsis. Instead, I found a cast listing, with Taneesha's name right on top. Why didn't she tell me? I threw it back in the corner when I heard the toilet flush; Taneesha was entitled to her secrets. *I just wish there hadn't been so many of them.*

※

One week, I couldn't find Taneesha. A job I was supposed to get never came through, so I was broke. I was afraid to go to the store and tell the man I didn't have any money. I hid out in my apartment and tried to figure out what to do. The rent was due in two weeks. I had been so sure I was going to get the job that I never made any contingency plans.

Pretty soon I forgot about the rent. I kept seeing myself in the leather jacket, cool and confident and beautiful. Not pretty, but beautiful. striking, even. I never had the kind of looks that people notice the first time, but Taneesha taught me how to draw attention to my eyes with eyeliner and emphasize my cheekbones with blush. People started to notice me. As soon as I had the jacket, I'd be complete. The jacket was all that mattered. But now it was lost to me. And I couldn't find Taneesha.

I wasn't worried when Taneesha first disappeared. She had done that before. Once, she'd gotten an understudy job in a play and disappeared for six days without telling me. She was like that. But she never missed a Saturday. Never.

Tuesday rolled around and I still hadn't heard from her. By Wednesday I was frantic. I hadn't seen nor heard from Taneesha now for a week and a half. I didn't know what to do. I lit some incense and paced my studio apartment from wall to wall. But my apartment was only seven steps wide, and I got dizzy. I stopped and sat on the couch. I put my head between my legs and tried not to cry. The money didn't matter. The jacket was lost. And Taneesha was gone.

I was on the verge of taking a deep breath when Taneesha walked into the room. I hadn't inhaled any oxygen yet, and my lungs froze. Taneesha ignored my shock. "You shouldn't leave the door unlocked," she said casually. "It's dangerous."

"The jacket, Taneesha," I said, "we lost the jacket. I couldn't put any money down this week." I started to cry. "Now I'll never have it. Everything is lost." I wasn't talking about the money. The jacket had transformed me. Without the hope of actually owning it, my new confidence started to wane. My shoulders began to slouch.

Taneesha's voice rang out like a shot. "Don't you understand?" She pulled a box from behind her back and lifted the lid. Even before I could see inside, I knew it was the jacket. Taneesha lifted it out and held it open for me with ceremony. I walked right into it.

I was so excited about the jacket, I never asked her how she got the money or where she had been for the past week and a half. I just assumed that she'd been working out some plot to get the jacket. It was only later that I found out she'd been in the hospital. I hadn't even known she was sick. They'd diagnosed her illness that weekend. The jacket was Taneesha's way of saying good-bye. *If only I had known it then.*

After Taneesha gave me the jacket, I wanted to do something nice for her, so I took her out to the desert. Since I didn't have a car, we hitched. We passed miles and miles of dry cacti and dead brush. I spotted bright colors in the distance and told the driver to stop. We got out of the car and I grabbed Taneesha's hand, forcing her to run with me. I didn't let her stop until we were in a field that looked like an impressionistic painting. The wildflowers had just started to bloom, and brilliant colors rippled across the terrain in the hot desert wind. Taneesha hadn't known there were flowers in the desert. It was nice to be able to show her something.

Taneesha stuck around for almost three months before she disappeared again. I wasn't worried at first, but when the time stretched from one week to two, I got a little concerned, and called her house, letting the phone ring. It was no big deal when Taneesha herself didn't answer, but when her answering machine didn't pick up, I knew something was drastically wrong — no actress ever leaves her phone unanswered.

I went to Taneesha's apartment and found her in bed. Her skin was pale and clammy, and she had lost a lot of weight. She sat up when I walked into the room, but I could see it was a struggle for her. She just didn't have any energy. I sat down on the bed, and she offered me a weak smile. It was a sort of apology. It wasn't for not calling — it was for dying. We both knew it.

Taneesha was going to die.

I don't know what came over me then. I screamed and yelled and threw things around the apartment. "Don't leave me, Taneesha!" I screamed. "Don't you dare leave me.

Bastards!" I accused, looking upward. "Why are you taking her?" I screamed until my throat was raw. Taneesha just lay there; she didn't even fight back. That scared me, so I hit her. Why wasn't she fighting?

It was hard to tell who started crying first. Suddenly we were in each other's arms, clinging in muted desperation. I was afraid to let go.

I didn't leave for almost two weeks. I stayed by Taneesha's side and fed her soup and bathed her. I read her stories when she couldn't sleep and mopped her forehead with a wet cloth when her fever got too high. I went out every morning to buy the newspaper. We both got a kick out of the advice columns. When Taneesha felt weak, I read them to her out loud.

She kicked me out when she started feeling better. She said she needed some time to herself. *She looked so much better. I trusted her.*

I didn't hear anything for three days. I was up late one night, just staring at the walls. I didn't feel like reading or watching TV. The vertical hold was broken anyway, and watching it gave me a headache.

At a quarter after twelve the phone rang. The ring was hollow. It sounded of death. I knew they were calling to tell me Taneesha was dead. The phone rang for a long time — I couldn't answer it.

After two days, I called the hospital. They said Taneesha's family had already flown her body home. I called Chicago from a pay phone and said I was Taneesha's friend. They said they had never heard of me, but they talked to me anyway. Taneesha had been cremated. They were sorry, but there wasn't going to be a memorial service. It would be too painful for everyone involved.

I sat in my apartment for a week and didn't move. No one came to my door. The phone didn't ring. Even my landlord left me alone.

On the eighth day, I put on the jacket and went outside. The sun hurt my eyes. I realized I had been sitting in the dark all week. I squinted until I got used to the light. Without being conscious of making a decision, I walked up to Hollywood Boulevard. Before I realized where I was, I had come to the spot where Taneesha and I had first met. I walked to the store where we got the jacket and looked in the window to see the man. I wanted to show him how I looked in the jacket, but he wasn't there. It was no good. I kept walking. When I found myself by the freeway, I started hitchhiking to the desert, to the place where the wildflowers bloomed, the place that belonged to Taneesha and me.

I got one ride all the way to the Mojave. I was in such a daze, I don't even remember who picked me up. I think it was a man in an old pickup, but I'm not really sure. I do remember that he asked me what exit I wanted. I told him I didn't know, I'd recognize it when I saw it. And I did. It was hot and dry. There weren't any wildflowers in February — I hadn't thought of that. But I could feel Taneesha there.

I started saying the Kaddish, the Jewish prayer for the dead, for my friend. I don't know where the words came from. The only time I'd said it before was when my grandmother died. I had only been thirteen at the time, so it was amazing that I remembered it. Taneesha wasn't even Jewish. I don't know if she was anything at all. She told me once that religion was all a crock. I wondered for a moment if God would punish me for saying a Jewish prayer for an atheist friend. I didn't think so — prayers are for the living.

I took the jacket off and laid it on the ground. The area was barren except for me, the jacket, and my memories of Taneesha. I knew then what I had to do. It was time to put Taneesha to rest.

I searched in the jacket pockets and pulled out a book of matches. I'm not sure why they were there, but they were.

I knew they would be. I built a small pile of sticks on the ground and lit them. They blazed immediately, and I threw the rest of the book in. I picked up the jacket and carefully placed it on the fire. As the flames licked upward, I stood up and said the comforting words from my childhood: *"Yis-ga-dal v'yis-ka-dash sh'may ra-bo..."* I knew Taneesha would understand.

AS IMPORTANT AS A LAMP

CAROL SEAJAY

Jean tensed and willed herself not to duck. *Just hold still,* she told herself. *Just hold still. Hold still.* But she ducked anyway. Behind her ear she heard Pat's fist slam into the cupboard door. Pat screamed with rage.

'*Why does it matter if* she *gets hurt, but it doesn't matter if* you *get hurt?*' The counselor's words rang in her mind with Pat's scream.

Not now. Not now. I don't have time for this now, Jean thought at the counselor and pushed her out of her mind, concentrating instead on the duck and the lunge that would push her past Pat in the moment before Pat recovered from the burst of pain in her hand and released this new fury on her.

Jean felt her muscles gather, pull together, then push. There! She was away, across the kitchen with her back to the stove. As she turned to face Pat, Pat was already screaming rage and moving toward her in cartoonlike slow motion. Her arms were raised in a lunge, reaching up, body lifting like a swimmer doing the butterfly stroke.

'You don't deserve this! You don't deserve to be hit!' came Elisa's voice. Elisa was the one counselor at the shelter who Jean listened to. The other counselors talked of leaving, of building new lives, of jobs. But Elisa talked about safety and the importance of surviving each attack. The anger in Elisa's voice held Jean's attention now.

"The rest of these namby-pamby counselors must live in fairy castles," Jean had joked to the other women at the shelter. But it had been too hard to stay there; everyone else was straight. "You let a *woman* do that to you!" Margarita, her roommate, couldn't get it. It wasn't clear to Jean whether Margarita had meant the battering or the sex. But the real difference was that Jean had no kids. "If I didn't have the kids, I'd just go," woman after woman had told her. So she went — back to Pat. Pat, who truly wanted her back, who promised that it would never happen again. But it did. It was happening right now.

Where the hell am I supposed to go? Jean wondered bitterly, as she watched Pat's slow-motion progress across the kitchen. The late-afternoon light streamed in through the window above the sink, crossing the narrow kitchen over the counter to the snack bar, inviting Jean to follow. If she were made of air, she could make it. With the clutter on the counter and the stools on the other side, there was no way she could follow the light's path. The only way out was the door behind Pat, who was still moving toward her.

'You don't deserve this!' Jean saw Elisa's fist pounding the tabletop, heard the genuine rage in her voice. *'You can't stop her from being angry, but* you *don't have to take it.'*

Jean chose. She chose Elisa's fist over Pat's. She ducked her head again, pushed off the range with one foot, and dived under Pat's descending butterfly-stroking arms. Pat's hands brushed her back. Feeling more than seeing Pat turn

132

in midair, she wished Pat was drunk so her response time would be slower and give her more time. But she made the kitchen door, pushed off with her hands again, and headed across the entryway. She leapt over the throw rug and was into the hallway when she heard Pat curse as she slipped on the rug. Riding on those few extra seconds, she made the bathroom, swung the door shut behind her, and pushed the button on the lock, the one lock in the whole damn house...

Pat screamed with frustrated rage and pounded on the door, her screams even more terrifying than before. Jean looked around the room with Elisa's eyes as Pat landed a kick on the flimsy door. The mirror — that was the worst. Pat might pound Jean's head against it, and the breaking glass could cut her badly. It could kill her. '*Whatever you do, stay alive,*' Elisa coached in her ear. The tub. She could fall in the tub and crack her skull. Or Pat could push her. Or shove her back into the sink, or either of them could fall over the toilet. Shit. This was the worst place she could be. Pat's third kick broke through the door. Time wasn't cooling her off at all.

Jean looked around the room desperately. The only way out was the window over the tub. Her trembling fingers finally freed the screen, and she pushed the casement open. She hoisted herself up, knocking shampoo bottles in all directions, twisted herself around, and dropped feet first to the ground below. She didn't need Elisa's voice in her ear to tell her to run as she heard Pat crash through the door.

Jean ran past the garage. '*Don't hide in the garage, that's the first place she'll look for you,*' Elisa's voice advised her. She ducked through the bushes that bordered their yard, crossed the street, ran up the hill, and ducked into a drainage culvert. She caught a breath and then, hiding behind a bush, peered out at the scene below — the house, the garage, the yard. The bathroom window was still flapping slowly.

Even at this distance she heard a crash in the house. Smaller, less frightening for the distance perhaps. But the distance didn't diminish the clarity with which she knew it was the lamp they had bought last weekend at the estate sale. So this wasn't the end of it. Pat was sealing something, Jean realized, as she listened with almost detachment to the subsequent crashes. The particular sound of things being swept off counters, off dressers with the pass of an arm. The crash of dishes. The almost waterfall sound of a smashed mirror raining to the floor. The demolition of all that would break in a home. There would be no going back this time.

She lay in the culvert listening, feeling more and more certain with each crash, but removed, as if she were watching her own house on television, hearing the crashes as if through the TV speaker. As if the distance created safety the way a TV screen did — you could be privy to violence and untouched at the same time.

She reviewed the action. The woman in the kitchen — herself — what if she hadn't ducked? What if she had absorbed the violence with her face? Taken the fist as Pat had expected? What if she hadn't run? Would the bathroom door have been broken down? The lamp crashed? The mirror shattered? But it was just as clear that if she had taken the blows, the lamp crashing would have happened inside her. Something inside her would have broken. Something as important and worthwhile as the lamp.

But it didn't matter now. The lamp was gone. It sounded as if the whole inside of the house was gone. She was gone, too. Jean kept waiting for Pat to storm out of the house, to come looking for her, but she didn't. Then she waited for Pat to storm out of the house, throw herself into the car and drive off, tires screeching around the hilly curves. Maybe she'd forget to lock the door and Jean could go back for her purse. She took inventory of her pockets: nothing except a phone message to call her mother. A lot of good that would do her! No money. Not even house keys.

The sun settled down into the hills. Dusk brought silence from the house below, but Pat didn't leave. When the dusk thickened into darkness, Jean crept down the hill, peered into neighbors' cars until she found a blanket, and carried it back up the hill to her vantage point. She wrapped it around herself and settled down to wait out the night. Pat would leave for work in the morning. Jean would make her way into the house, get her purse and some clothes, keys, the checkbook ... She visualized her purse on the table in the entryway. Pity she hadn't grabbed it as she ran for the bathroom. If she had, she could be on her way now.

It was a while before she realized that with all the smashing and throwing of things and the sweeping of things off counters, her purse would no longer be sitting on the table. She began to imagine the clutter on the floor. The smashed dishes littering the kitchen floor. The lamp shards scattered across the carpet. The photo of her and Pat in its stand-up frame that sat on the entryway table, with Pat radiating pride and love and Jean happier than she'd ever been in her life. No doubt it was victim of the rampage, too. Jean saw it smashed on the floor, her purse, the contents scattered across the room, empty beside it.

Then she realized that Pat wouldn't get up in the morning and go to work. She'd wait for Jean to come crawling back. There was no point in waiting any longer. Jean picked herself up and felt her way down the hill in the darkness. Someone would give her dimes for a phone call. Elisa might not be at the shelter, but someone would be there. They would let her stay the night. Elisa would come eventually, and when she did, she would know what to do next. Even better than that, Elisa would be glad that Jean had left.

Better than glad! Jean imagined looking into Elisa's deep brown eyes and saying, "This time is different. I'm not going back this time. I finally got it." She imagined Elisa being glad for her. With her. Imagining that, Jean began to feel glad herself. She was walking now, past the house, down the hill, toward the future. Not a cent in her pocket, no lover by her side, but something like a grin on her face and a new confidence in her step.

WOOD BURNING

KATHLEEN M. QUINLAN

This is the part about her you'll find the strangest: I mean her being a Welcome Wagon lady with her prison record and all. Claims she's innocent as a baby's butt. Still, there are those who question just how it is she's one of the few in town to afford an electric garage door and one of those all-night bug executioners. They don't come cheap, and we've most of us come on hard times with this economy all tied up by the sheiks.

Even claims her mother was D.A.R., but that she never had the inclination toward public displays of being highborn and pledging allegiance and the like.

I began to think all of this was just to put me on when she told me about the paternity of that woolly-haired child she drags around town. Insists he's Irish as Dublin. Named the boy McGinty for the man she, shall we say, was "widowed" from. I'd have called him Booker T. Now, she goes by her maiden name on account of it pleasing her late father, General Whatsisname.

Believe me, I'm not one to doubt the word of a God-fearing woman, but there's something about when she lets you in on this or that piece about herself, that you'd swear she's making up every stitch of it and laughing right in your face.

Still, I find myself interested, you might say, in hearing more. I goes right on giving her the benefit of the doubt, admitting that woolly-haired boy into the Bible Day Camp I run, and even come out dressed to the gills for the opening of her café up near the mall.

I get there to find her in blue jeans and those striped rubber-soled shoes. Granted, the apron did give her a look of having some sensible feelings toward sanitation. Turns out the place is geared toward the improvement of your health. If she thinks some biker's going to pull off the interstate for a helping of that tofu business she tried to stuff down me, she might as well lock the door and live off the county.

And I don't mind telling her straight out that she'd better get something edible on this menu if she intends to turn a profit. Now don't get me wrong. She's worked hard on it. That's plain enough. It's all put down in those fancy italic letters, but after all, she lives on the lot right next to mine and when her place goes to seed — well, you get the picture.

She sits down at my table, and I congratulate her on the arrangement of fresh flowers. I lean in a little so as to be able to say in a low tone about the menu, and up she comes with that flashy-toothed smile of hers like I'm the one's touched.

She tells me she's not hoping to draw the bikers and that it's a "women's restaurant." Frank and I have driven that camper from here to Fairfax and never once saw a sign announcing food that only women can digest. I look back on the menu and try to be of comfort, telling her that Frank and the kids could probably get down the number four — the Fish Fillets in Sesame Sauce.

Now, she's laughing, but it's a laugh that looks like she's happy for my suggestions — like she even likes me some. So I sally forth with more, like about getting a jukebox. If you can believe this, she vetoes the idea and informs me about a group of her women friends who have a string quartet. She's going to have one evening a week just for women to get together for the purpose of conversation.

I wait and wait for Frank to get home to tell him about this new enterprise of our neighbor. He's doing well in construction. Put me in a four-bedroom central air and Momma in her own Florida trailer with patio-porch. Listen, life is good for me, real good. I have a Lincoln that gets me to and from. I'm steady at the hairdresser. The boys are straight of limb and keep their marks to what Frank expects. They've got the Nintendo, and, Lord, I've got clothes I don't even recollect the purchase of. Even have an investment now, part ownership in the Bible Day Camp. Knock wood, more than I ever hoped for.

Anyway, I'm cutting the fat off Frank's T-bone and telling him about the café. All he says is, "Dykes — a bunch of bulldykes." I drop myself into the chair, staggered at the thought that I ate the actual food of dykes, and instantly become queasy.

Later, when Frank covers me with himself and takes his fill just like I wanted him to with his T-bone, I'm thinking — God forgive me — yes, about dykes. Frank is all excited and here I am asking myself, Why do women want to do this with each other? "Want to do what?" I say aloud. Frank mumbles something. And the pictures that come into my mind — well, I turned to prayer that instant, hoping the pictures were a result of the dyke food I ingested, and promised God never never to eat tutu again. Frank rolls over and pats his belly like he's had too much apple Danish.

Next morning, I vow to rip McGinty right out of Bible Day Camp. While formulating just how to put it, I watch him learning crafts. Wouldn't you just know it — he's making a present for her. With the wood-burning set, he painstakingly prints his poor twisted mother's Christian name across the top of a cedar box.

The counselor has spelled it out on paper for him so he'll shape the letters right — K-A-T-H-L-E-E-N. Lord, this could take a week or more. I'm about to tell him to never board the camp van again, but I get the idea that he might as well stay on with us and learn a trade. All right, he is only six and wood burning won't get him far. I know that, but I've read things at the hairdresser about children learning manual dexterity, which will advance them in later life. I let it go, that's all. Besides, what's it to you, anyway?

In no time at all I'm sweeping Indiana's autumn from the porch. Kathleen comes up the walk looking at me like I'm kin and telling me how the café's doing well. I nearly had to work my face manually just to muster a neighborly look of greeting. She'd like to build on an addition and wonders if Frank would be interested in bidding.

When reminded of his sentiments about the patrons of this place, he says, "I don't care if they're orangutans long as they intend to foot the bill."

Since I do all the book work for the business, I was forced to stop at the café from time to time while construction was in progress. The only day good for me to go over is Monday, when Frank's home with the football and can look out for the boys. It's just as well, because the kitchen's closed on Mondays. Nobody there but that talk group.

Sometimes, I listen to the blend of voices. Don't ask me why, but now and then the sound gives me a feeling of energy like every Christmas when I hear "Good King Wenceslas."

One night as I'm taking a cabinet measurement back in the kitchen, I can't help but overhearing them. Kathleen, my neighbor, is saying about feeling angry, about being treated like trash as a lesbian, about the trials and joys of raising little McGinty.

Something, only God knows what, makes me walk out there and sit down. Maybe just curiosity to get an eyeful of what an assembly of dykes looks like. In soft tones an older woman is talking about her need to feel family around her. And get this, of all odd notions, how in this godforsaken college town, this group has become her family. That she's looking forward to the holidays with them this year.

I cannot take another word. I stand up like I'd been called on in a school class and give out my name. Let them put it in the *Guardian* for all I care. Someone's got to infiltrate this congregation of — of … Someone had better set them toward sense.

"I am Mrs. Frank L. Chandler. My friends call me Dorothy Chandler, and I am here tonight to say you make me sick unto death. You want respect? You want family? Well, get your backsides out of here and go get yourselves some real love. Get yourself a man like Frank. From the day of my nuptials to this, I have wanted for nothing. Respect? Friends? There's not a woman in this county wouldn't put elbow grease to any project I've a mind to undertake if I asked her." And I go on some more. I let them know.

Now, I hear my voice getting louder. My knees begin to weaken, probably from the weight of public speaking, and tears are blurring up my eyes. Damned if one of those dykes don't come across the room and wrap her arms around me like I was one of their persuasion. Surely, it is fear of her or them. For all I know, they bear arms. Whatever — I'm crying, sobbing, like I never did in my lifetime. But this woman don't seem to mind. She just kind of rocks me and says my name a lot.

Just as I regain my composure, right in front of them all she says, "Is it that you're lonely, Dorothy?"

She looks at me so close, as if my answer really matters. I never saw anyone look at me so careful before, so close. As I study her eyes, it seems as if I can suddenly see all the faces I'd ever looked on. I can see what's been missing in every one of them. Never a "Is it that you're lonely, Dorothy?" Never a "Is it anything, Dorothy?"

Seems I must have talked aloud an hour or more — crazy things. Things I can't remember thinking before. About how I knew everyone but no one knew me and then later, about how I knew no one — no one really at all.

I make Frank wake up when I get home. "Look at me, Frank. Look at me a minute. Please, Frank." And I look in his eyes. I look harder than I ever looked at anything or anyone.

Nowhere do his eyes say, "Is it that you're lonely, Dorothy?"

I search through the moonlight in the room thinking I'll steady myself with sights of what is mine, but nothing here is mine. Not the man, not the rose wallpaper, not the room.

Finally, when I close my eyes, I discover that I can take full possession of the first thing I ever really owned — the look in the eyes of that good woman who saw all of Dorothy — the look of someone who saw me.

Don't know how long I lay there engraving that look in me, searing it to last like a name burned into a cedar box.

UNANNOUNCED

ELAINE J. AUERBACH

For the first time since Helen's death from cancer two years ago, Marion dared to make a real commitment. It wasn't to a person, which didn't strike her as strange at the time, but to a house. After having lived in her own separate apartment throughout their twenty-year relationship, she bought a house in Provincetown and moved there for the summer.

"Marion's finally had it with being in the closet," Lorna, one of Helen's closest friends, hinted at a Fourth of July party after Marion's departure to the Cape for the season. "Too bad Helen's not around to see it."

Lorna was only one of a group of friends who had stood by while Helen struggled with Marion's insistence on remaining in the closet. Helen had always been the risky one, excited by change, eager to be fashionable, while Marion retained her fifties conservatism, preferring quiet dinners with friends and nondescript, unostentatious modes of dress. Helen had put up a strong resistance. She had tried numerous times to bring her lover up to date, sewing colorful and revealing skirts, jumpsuits, and jackets for Marion to wear. Entering the world without Helen's hand-iwork, Marion would go unnoticed; with it, she became a jewel, the bright purples, yellows, oranges, and blues setting off her light sandy hair and coal black eyes. Marion was tall, commanding in stature, and when she dressed in Helen's creations her figure would evoke the kind of attention traditionally reserved for those in uniform, for it was evident to those who knew Marion well that she wore the seams and stitches with a pride that came from fidelity to her lover — to something beyond herself.

Marion didn't hear any of the gossip about her. In any event, she would have found it absurd. She hadn't bought the house because she wanted to "come out." And she really had no desire to socialize with the "townies," those artistic and commercially minded gays who made P-town their permanent home. She was accustomed to her closeted existence, and, at fifty-three years of age, she didn't see that she had much to gain by being carefree and open in a gay ghetto. She had bought the house because of the tree.

❇

The red cedar grew within ten feet of the front door, its feathery branches bursting to fullness in the free air above the roof. Healthy. Sovereign. It thrived on sources that, no matter how observant Marion was, were invisible to the naked eye. The small garden surrounding the tree sprouted forget-me-nots, wild violets, primroses, and a small juniper bush whose aroma mingled with its larger cousin the cedar. The fresh scent of the cedar and the budding life of the garden formed a natural place of meditation, a welcoming entrance to the weathered-gray clapboard house.

144

The house had once been a Portuguese fisherman's shack, moved a century before to safer ground, from the pier that had since been claimed by the ocean.

But the ground *wasn't* safe. Marion read in a tourist guidebook that around 1940 the Cape had measured twelve miles across at the tip. Since then, nearly nine miles had been swallowed by the ocean. The simple fact was that her house was dangerously perched on a three-mile spread of dune that could easily be swept away.

Marion saw a connection between the status of her house and the supposedly strong foundations of understanding and acceptance of the gay community in P-town, a foundation that fell each year during the annual Labor Day gay-bashing weekend. She realized that the tree, towering at a height of more than fifty feet, unable to forecast and escape from threatening influences, continued to thrust its hungry roots into the slipping sands, yearning for growth and survival against all odds, against the buffeting sea winds, the salt-laden air, the slowly eroding coastline. The life of the tree, silently growing, oblivious to impending dangers, was impossible to ignore. Marion cherished the tree's lack of consciousness just as she did her memories of Helen, believing that her memories would escape the destructive effects of time and circumstance.

The house required repair and renovation, inside and out. The downstairs rooms and the attic seemed imper-manent, as if made of cardboard rather than wood, lacking proper finishing and insulation. The scarred pinewood floors bore the imprints of many footsteps, imprints whose history Marion unintentionally discovered.

"Ye-es," Marty the postman meandered with his words, "your place's seen a lot of activity, all right, but not as much as you'd think. Only one family ever lived there after it was moved from the pier. The Flynns. Eddie Flynn came down from Boston and married a local girl from Brewster. They settled here, round about, oh, I'd say late 1800s. Maybe a bit earlier."

Marion didn't ask Marty how he knew what he knew. His husky body, steel blue eyes, and graying beard cast him in the role of the sage advisor, someone who could be trusted for at least a fair semblance of truth. After all, she couldn't doubt a postman, a person who had made a living being reliable.

"They lived in the original shack?"

"That's right, moved into the shack but did some work, as I understand. Expanded the place, because they planned on having a family. Must have about four rooms now, is that right?"

"No. Three in the attic and three downstairs, not counting the kitchen and bath."

"Oh, yes, that many? Hmm. Must be quite comfortable for you there."

Was he suggesting that he knew she was alone? Was he thinking that maybe she was gay? Marion ignored the implication of his comment, telling herself that men were always confused by the notion of a woman living on her own.

"Well, Mr. O'Brien, I'll have to do some research on the place."

"You can do that," he advised, "by visiting Doris Hines at Town Hall. She runs the heritage committee. Can tell you the history of practically every nook and cranny on this part of the Cape."

Marion politely thanked him for his advice, telling herself she wasn't interested in Doris prying into her life. 'Oh,' she could hear Doris say, 'you're the new owner of the Flynn place. And what do you do and where are you from and are you married...' The possibilities were endless and endlessly tiresome for Marion.

She never expected Doris Hines would come to her, but this is just what she did on hearing from Marty O'Brien about

146

Marion's arrival. Marion was reading in the living room on a late Saturday afternoon when she heard a timid rapping at the door. She looked up to see a shadowed figure peering at her through the screen.

Marion rarely ventured beyond her house and yard, except for the occasional walk to the store at the corner or to the beach after sunset, eschewing contact with the town. Yet here was a representative of the town, a singular invasion of her privacy.

As she approached the door, Marion gradually made out that the figure was a woman, probably in her late seventies. She was small, a round body on thin, thin legs. Her thick hair was tinted a brilliant carrot red.

"I hope I'm not intruding," her cheery voice intoned, "but I heard you had just moved in. I'm Doris Hines."

Doris Hines was intrusive, and chatty, but restrained enough not to probe Marion about her life. Doris's main interest was relating her knowledge of the past for the edification of those living in the present.

"Eddie Flynn was a lobsterman. Off on the boats a lot those days. He didn't have much time for family matters, it would seem, though he and Mrs. Flynn had fifteen children. They were all delivered here by the midwife, Mrs. Dawes. Eddie died just after the last one was born. Terrible. A real burden for Mrs. Flynn, bringing up all those children. And in her later years, well, you know how forgetful children can be."

Spoken from her experience as a mother? Marion wondered. She waited, expecting Doris to unravel stories about her own family, but this didn't happen.

"I admired Mrs. Flynn," Doris continued. "We were good friends. I learned a lot from her, believe me. She died when she was nearly a hundred years old. House stood empty for years until her heirs decided to sell it off. She had a lot of spunk in her. A fighter till the day she died. Took on the town when they wanted to axe that fine cedar tree in front of the house because, they said, it was interfering with the new electric wires. Mrs. Flynn wanted electricity, mind you, but she wanted the electricity *and* the tree."

"The tree was almost cut down?"

"Yup. But Mrs. Flynn saved it. Had them move all the poles to the other side of the road where there weren't any trees. Wasn't that an accomplishment? Do you like that cedar? You aren't thinking of chopping it down, now?"

"No, not at all. I fell in love with that tree in spite of the house."

Doris Hines laughed. "Well, that's a really surprising thing to say. Very surprising for a change. But I guess it's the influence of the younger folks, all concerned about saving the earth, stopping the bombs. They make me feel that life is still worth living. They're not all taking drugs, are they? There's still hope, isn't there?"

She was pleading with Marion, asking for some reassurance that all her record keeping wasn't being done in vain. The young were the answer to everything. They were everyone's last resort, the final solution to their elders' unsolved problems.

Marion was relieved when Doris got up, apologized for taking up her time, and left as suddenly as she had arrived. After Doris's departure, Marion imagined Mrs. Flynn scowling at the Grim Reaper, in noble New England style, from where she sat beneath the cedar on a warm summer's day, protected by the one she had saved from a premature death. She wondered if Mrs. Flynn had been pleased with the tiled bathroom that replaced the outhouse and the porcelain range that supplanted the wood stove. Surely she had welcomed the electric lights that bathed her in a continuous glow by which she could gaze, unobstructed by shadows of indecision and uncertainty, into the faces of her children, grandchildren, and great-grandchildren, into the faces of hope.

A fulfilled woman. A woman fulfilling her biological destiny.

One destiny for one life. A deceptively simple compromise. A cruelly simple correspondence.

But hadn't she made just such a pact with fate, committing herself to one woman for twenty years, having in the end simply a storehouse of memories, with nothing to pass on, to mark their brief space upon the earth in the eons of time passing? What kind of hope did she have left? A deceptively simple correspondence, her relationship with Helen: "Remain with me as long as mortality lasts, my dear." When mortality ended, where was destiny?

✳

Marion first saw Mrs. Flynn in the pantry, stacking and restacking provisions for her family. She moved slowly, with calm deliberation. Her hair was dark and streaked with gray; she wore a blue dress and an apron trimmed in lace. Having never seen a ghost before, Marion was terrified at first. Her immediate inclination was to go to someone — anyone — and plead for assistance. But what kind of assistance would she ask for? Was she in danger? No. Then what help did she need? Was she seeing things? Maybe. Could this mean she was going insane? She refused to believe that her usual clearheadedness was failing her. No, she couldn't be crazy. When she heard Mrs. Flynn's deep sighing before she opened the latch on the pantry door, a sound that was indrawing as well as expelling, she remembered Helen's labored breathing, her excruciating pain. Marion sympathized with the presence. For more than a week she asked questions of Mrs. Flynn, about her life, her children, about Doris Hines, but received only more sighs. Eventually the spirit no longer appeared in the pantry, and Marion thought she had exorcised her presence.

But one night, idle and isolated from all the familiars of her life in the city; and contemplating the alterations she could make to the house, Marion saw the pale reflection of Mrs. Flynn trapped in the living room window, her straight white teeth forming a piteous smile, begging release. Marion's initial terror was reawakened by the visitation. Caught between her uncertainty about whether these were hallucinations or reality, she was unable to make any alterations to the house. The sparsest of means, aligned to the barest of needs, was evident wherever she looked — in the wiring that was tacked to the baseboards, in the rickety wooden ladder to the attic, in the unmatched flowered paper covering the walls. The house was infused with the character of its former owner, unlike the cedar tree, which evidenced no mortal touch.

Were her relationships fashioned like the house? Looking back on her years with Helen, she saw how her most basic needs had governed their choice of friends and activities. The overwhelming conventions of society had restrained them from acting contrary to the limits Marion had established for them as a couple. In a short two years, she had negated her attachment to Helen, replacing the empty socket of devotion with her teaching duties at the college; she had entrenched herself in a basic survival mentality, her sexual orientation safely yet clandestinely rooted.

She had been expected to invite friends for a weekend on the Cape, but she always found a way to avoid extending the invitation. Only Sandra, a friend with contacts of her own in P-town, circumvented Marion's plans for exclusion. She showed up one afternoon in early August. Marion was embarrassed, for she had led everyone to believe she was working hard on the house, getting it in shape for visitors next summer, and here was Sandra, witness to the still-splitting trim on the archway, the sagging ceiling, the peeling paint.

"Well, it has potential. When are you going to start work on it?" Sandra questioned, eyeing Marion's unkempt, graying hair, her frayed and wrinkled shirt and pants.

"I don't think I'm going to do much, actually."

"Short on cash?" Sandra said, flipping her tortoise-shell glasses up and down on her head.

"Well, yes," Marion lied. Why not lie to someone like Sandra, the successful real estate agent? Sandra was a person who believed that economics was at the root of everything. She could understand money, or what was worse, not having money.

"Hey, look. I have this young friend — she's just a friend — who's very handy with tools and very low on cash herself. You could barter with her — a place to stay for some handiwork. What do you say?"

Marion didn't answer, allowing the conversation to drift to other matters. But when Cynthia arrived ten days later, in the middle of the night, unannounced, Marion wished she had refused Sandra's offer outright.

"Hi, I'm Cynthia," a young woman, no more than twenty, with hair black and curly and clothing leathery and spectral, declared as she deposited an orange tabby cat with the rest of her gear on the kitchen floor.

"Cynthia?"

"Didn't Sandra phone you? She said she would. I'm the one who's handy dandy and willing to trade labor for a few other favors."

With this introduction, she winked at Marion. The playful, though provocatively teasing, gesture was something Helen had been fond of doing with new acquaintances to ease tension and establish contact.

Marion doubted that Sandra would commit such an oversight. More likely this "baby dyke" couldn't wait for confirmation before she demanded fulfillment of her needs. The needs of youth, of those struggling to survive, always held paramount importance. Style was the most important thing to youth, or at least to those who kept youth in the forefront of their lives. She saw it so often in the college students, girls and boys who copied each other, so firmly entrenched in the present that they missed the most obvious changes in their own experience. They had no time to recollect. Helen had been that way, eager to keep pace with a changing world, as if the world could get beyond her, which, tragically, it had succeeded in doing. Helen hadn't been able to beat it. Marion was conscious of how she had given up on trying to outrun the forward motion of time. Cynthia was just beginning the marathon.

"I'll call Sandra tomorrow," Marion responded coldly, consciously displaying her most supercilious look. "As long as you're here, you might as well take one of the upstairs rooms."

"Super! This is a great place. You'll have to tell me all about it tomorrow. I'm hitting the beach first thing in the morning — have to catch some sun and see some women, if you know what I mean — but I'll be back by noon."

"There's a presence in this house," Marion said, acting herself like a ghost annoyed by the intrusion of such an obviously living personality.

Gathering her bags and heading up the ladder to the attic, Cynthia didn't appear to hear what Marion said, which was just as well, because Marion couldn't believe she had actually admitted her visions to a stranger. Was she losing herself, going completely bonkers? Maybe it *was* better not to be alone in this house. She went to bed, thinking how unusual it was to be sharing her space with a flesh-and-bone guest instead of an apparition.

That night Marion had a dream. Cold surrounded her feet, her legs, her waist, her breasts, and finally her head. The air had become water. She walked through water, breathing through her ears, eyes, every orifice of her body.

She saw the house, solid but wavering, and Cynthia's cat above the chimney, a furry, wingless bird. Helen swam next to her, a phosphorescent fish, gilt with shimmering silver clouds, trailing a stream of rainbow bubbles. Marion caught her breath at the beauty, suddenly becoming anxious and gasping for air. Where was the cedar? What had happened to the cedar tree? It was gone! She saw the house, unshaded, exposed, and the cedar torn out by the roots, caught in the vortex of a current that grew ever warmer and more powerful, gradually overcoming the cold encasing her body.

The next morning, stunned by her dream, Marion decided to go for a walk into town. While she was dressing, her eye strayed to a half-open trunk next to her dresser. Some of the precious clothes Helen had made for her lay within. She ached to feel Helen again, to hear her voice, to touch her warm, living skin. She wanted to cry out, to scream, "Mrs. Flynn, I, too, am an old woman, living alone in this forsaken house!" Instead, she dressed herself in one of Helen's favorite outfits, a turquoise jumpsuit, delighting in the caress of the material, a remnant of her lover's spirit.

As soon as she left the house, her mood changed. She felt threatened and wanted to keep to the bay side of the town, perhaps head toward Race Point and the beaches, avoiding the crowds of people along Commercial Street — gay couples, male and female, walking arm-in-arm, clutching each others' bodies in stolen acts of pleasure. How they flaunted their lives, oblivious as the cedar to the powers poised to destroy them!

She was safe, Marion told herself. She was trapped and lost and lonely, but she was safe. Why court danger? She had courted Helen. Had Helen, then, been dangerous? Sweet, gentle Helen. So much suffering, too horrendous a death for one who loved life so much. Helen as a threat to her existence? She shuddered at the implications of her own paranoid logic.

Marion found herself veering from her preferred direction. Head lifted, gaze on the passersby, she entered the flow of people moving toward the Town Hall area in the sparkling brilliance of the early-morning sun. She was awed by the number of gay men and women lining the streets. As she approached a straight couple, ready as ever to make room for them to go by on the slim sidewalk, she was amazed when they parted to allow her to pass between them.

She was visible.

She hadn't announced to everyone, "Hello, I'm Marion, I'm a math instructor, and I'm a lesbian!" They knew who she was. Who was she trying to kid? She dug into the pockets of her jumpsuit, feeling for Helen's hands in the fibers, wishing now she had listened to Helen's needs instead of her own fear.

It was too late, she sadly realized. Her fear had been that strong.

Marion returned home in the late afternoon to hear a loud banging coming from the living room. Passing beneath the cedar, she felt a spasm of anxiety travel through her.

Cynthia was tearing apart the living room walls. Marion was certain she was dismantling the house.

"What on earth are you doing?" Marion shouted, shaking with anger.

Cynthia, in jeans and sweatshirt, her hair pulled back in a conservative bun that made her look perversely mature, stared at the formidable older woman.

"I got back from the beach earlier than I thought I would — not much action there, I mean, everybody's sleeping off last night — so I thought I'd get to work on the insulation. These walls are going to need a lot of packing. How about you telling me more about the history of this place while I get on with the job?"

"Don't you think you should have asked me before you started this work? Don't you have any sense of responsibility

154

or courtesy? First you march in here, unannounced and, to my mind, uninvited, and now—"

"I thought you wanted some help—"

"I think you'd better go pack your bags. I don't need this."

"No, *you* might not, but the house does. I've been doing some inspecting. If you don't insulate and fix up some of those leaks on the roof and get rid of the dry rot you already have, the whole place is going to collapse around you. Houses need work. They don't maintain themselves like that cedar outside."

"You don't miss a trick, do you?" Marion remarked.

"I try not to. By the way, where'd you get that jumpsuit? It looks good on you. I like the color."

"If it's any of your business, someone very dear made it for me."

"I guess if she hadn't, you'd be running around naked, right?"

For an instant, Marion thought she saw the reflection of Mrs. Flynn in a beam of light that entered through the window by the fireplace and swept in a gold stream across Cynthia's youthful, smiling face.

The living and the dead, the young and the old, all of these together, Marion saw, mingled to create hope. "The future," she remembered Helen saying, "is now."

Marion felt a surge of renewal, of sudden courage. The times were forever changing. Trees needed protection. No house took care of itself. It wasn't all up to her, but in a deeper sense, it was.

Marion watched as Cynthia tore another section from the wall. She walked over to the younger woman, a destiny in the making, and knew she would never see Mrs. Flynn again.

155

ROBYN

NONA M. CASPERS

Julie stood outside the door. She rubbed one finger against the top of the steel handle and watched her face swim in the metal. Her eyes were red and swollen from driving and crying for three days straight. She looked up at the pictures taped to the synthetic-wood door — Gary Cooper, Cary Grant, Faulkner, Hemingway, Jesus, and Kermit the Frog hovered like clouds over a picture of a young man in a tight red-sequined dress, black pompadour, high painted cheekbones, big red lips, and long lashes on a pale face.

Who was he supposed to be? she wondered. Robyn never would tell her. Julie remembered the black play wig she'd gotten for her seventh birthday — he'd begged to wear it. They had both wanted black hair, not blond. And god, they'd had fun sneaking into the top bathroom drawer full of makeup and jewelry and scarves.

The rest of the pictures on the door were of men she didn't recognize, had never met. Julie interrogated their expressions and her own tightened into a fist. She hugged her elbows.

"I am not going to think like this," she reminded herself, and taking a deep breath, she pushed open the door. The room was dimly lit — a yellowing fluorescent light flickered above the hospital bed. Robyn lay on top of the sheets on his back, facing the window. He wore the red silk pajamas she'd sent him at Easter. His long skinny legs reached the footboard; one hand was draped above his head, fingers still, while the other tapped out some song on the boiled and bleached sheets. Some old Jagger or Bowie verse, Julie guessed. The fingers of that hand reminded her of an old man's.

God, look at him, she thought, he looks like he's spent the last year in a damp cell. No wonder Nan didn't want to come with her.

"Hi, sis." Robyn spoke quietly, without interrupting his view.

Julie let out her breath. "Hello." Damn, he's not going to make this easy. He had never made it easy.

The light flickered over him, haloing his brittle hair and gray skin for brief moments.

"Aren't you going to tell me I should have knocked?"

"I don't have time to tell people things they already know," he said. Robyn turned his head slowly toward her, as if he could hear the tear which slid from her cheek. He watched her face intently, like he used to watch the rain from their front porch. Julie let him watch — there was no place to hide in this small sterile room. And there was no time.

Suddenly Robyn's eyes changed. He looked her up and down, the old way, critiquing her for fashion.

"You look butch."

"Don't tell me that. I'm a femme."

"How's Nan?"

157

"Okay. She couldn't come with, she has a lot of work to do. But she sends her love."

Robyn squinted at her in disbelief and mumbled, "Wouldn't want her to miss a rally." Then, louder, "Think you'll survive without her for a whole week?"

"I don't know. It's an experiment."

"Risky," he said, and turned back to the window. The day outside hung cold and gray. Julie wished she could hand him a pill and walk away. Drive home and curl up in Nan's safe fleshy arms. Forget she had a brother. That's what she'd been doing. Now that he was in front of her, she couldn't pretend. But what could she do? He'd stopped listening to her advice when he hit puberty.

Robyn's spidery fingers tapped — it was a simple rhythm. His cheekbone stuck out like a pyramid. He'd always wanted to be rich and travel; she'd always wanted to rescue people from floods and villains, making them forever grateful, loyal. They'd played for whole days, acting out their dreams with their dolls. She had Calamity Jane on a polka-dot horse; he had Bunsen Bernie with a Paris chef hat and grill. She'd been allowed to go on playing with dolls, while he was launched into the world of football, basketball, and hockey.

He'd been a good little gay jock, she thought. Even the last time she'd seen him, he'd been full of energy and muscle, dancing until his sweat spattered her face. Such a damn good dancer. Wasted on men whose idea of a long-term relationship was three good fucks. Then Julie remembered — Robyn was one of those men. What had happened to the devoted little boy who played dolls with her?

Julie took a step closer to the bed. "Robyn...," she began the apology she'd planned in the car: *I'm sorry it's taken me so long to come here. I don't have a good excuse. I just didn't want to see you, like this.* But Robyn continued looking out the window, and the words grew stale in her stomach. She

158

noticed that his feet joined in the rhythm now, along with his fingers, against the bedboard. He wore different-colored socks — bright orange and a deep rose.

"I like your socks." She imitated the way he talked to her sometimes, in his fashion-conscious voice.

Robyn looked down and wiggled his toes. "Gifts from my last two lovers."

Julie tried to smile, but couldn't, and he knew. The fluorescent light flickered over the white walls, Robyn tapped, pigeons landed on the black roof outside the window, then flew away and landed again.

"Not much of a view."

"I like it. I get to watch the pigeons crap all over."

Julie tried again. "So, do any of your friends come?"

"Oh, they come all over the place — can't keep a good man dry," Robyn answered wickedly, like the kid she knew in high school who loved to shock everyone, and did.

Julie suddenly wanted to grab him by those ghostly shoulders and shake his pretty white teeth loose, to shake him like a little boy and scream, "How am I supposed to get you out of this mess?" as though he were being kept after school for sassing, or smoking cigarettes. Then she heard herself say what she wasn't going to say, this time.

"You and your goddamn sacred promiscuity. Your holy fucks. Everything's got to be sexualized. Why? Look where those holy encounters with those holy men have gotten you, you stupid ass. And where are all those holy men now? Off fucking someone else — 'coming all over the place,' huh? What the hell were you thinking all this time, Robyn? What did you get out of it?"

Robyn lay still as death, then rolled carefully onto his side to face her. His milky blue eyes were slightly out of focus, and wet. He spoke like someone who was going to say it one last time.

"I have enjoyed my lovers, and my body, and my holy fucks. I wasn't hunting for someone to cling to forever and ever, all right?" Taking a shaky breath, he faced the ceiling. "And I don't have time to listen to your latent-right-wing-lesbian lore and morals just now. So get off your polka-dot horse, I happen to be dying and I need a sister."

Julie could hear the pain rattle in his throat and felt her own burn. Before she could speak, the door flew open and a nurse appeared with meds. She wore a paper mask and plastic gloves. After Robyn swallowed the pills in the paper cup she checked his pulse. Julie watched the young woman avoid her brother's eyes and hold his wrist as if it were a python. He mumbled, "Don't worry, I won't bite or spit." The nurse glanced nervously around the room, then rested her gaze on Julie with relief.

"Oh. You two look alike," she said, happily surprised.

"We're sisters." Julie smiled at the bare eyes above the mask and heard Robyn laugh. The nurse offered an unsure smile, scribbled something on a tiny piece of white paper, and left.

Julie watched the door float shut, then slowly moved to sit in the plastic chair close to the bed. Her chin was level with Robyn's sunken chest, which rose and fell like a tired sea. Looking up at his face, she remembered his first day of school at Saint Mary's — how she'd found him at the back of the church crying. How she took his hand and brought him to his teacher. How he didn't want to let go. She thought of saying, "Robyn, when you get out of here ... if you get out of here again, why don't you come stay with me and Nan?" But she didn't.

"Robyn?" She searched for his eyes and tried to remember if in these last five years she'd told him that she loved him. When had it become so hard?

"Yes?" he questioned back, waiting. Julie leaned forward and rested her tired head lightly on the edge of his bed. She

160

felt his hand touch her short curls and twist them around his fingers, one finger tracing the triangle she had shaved on top.

"I like this," Robyn said approvingly. The light flickered over Julie's eyes, painting soft yellow stars under each lid. Other people talked in other rooms, murmuring like crickets in a jar.

After what seemed like a long while, she spoke, keeping her eyes safely shut. "Robyn, if you need anything from me," she began, not sure what she was trying to say, but knowing now was the time to say it, "I mean, if there's something you want me to hear, or do — or that you need to hear from me..." Julie opened her eyes and they looked at each other the way she imagined they could long ago. Robyn's face was calm and serious.

"I have three questions," he said, and held up three fingers. When they were little, Julie told him that she knew everything. So he'd bring her questions, and she'd make up the answers.

Julie sat up straight. "What are they?"

Holding up one finger, he asked, "Is there a hell?"

"No. There is no hell. Next question."

Robyn popped up a second finger. "Is it going to hurt, to die?"

Julie grabbed his aged hand and squeezed. "The pain will go away, and it will be like flying. You'll see Paris and Berlin and Nepal and Zurich and Newark, New Jersey. Then you'll get to dance with Cary Grant and Faulkner and Kermit the Frog. And Gertrude Stein," she added, "for me."

"Will I see you around?"

"Oh, yes. All lesbians are sent to the Riviera. We're the chosen people." They laughed, and Robyn had to catch his breath.

"Now," he said, no longer serious, "for the hard question."

"Your three are up."

"No, that last one was an unplanned child," he bickered weakly.

"Okay, okay, since you're in the hospital I'll let you get by."

He looked smug. "If you can guess this song, I'll bequeath you my red-sequined Chiquita Banana dress."

"You will? Really?" Julie had asked him for it every time she'd seen him these last five years.

"Would I lie on my deathbed?" he punned. Julie thought the medication must be working.

"I don't know," she answered truthfully.

"Well, I may, but I'm not."

Julie frowned. "Chiquita Banana? Is that who you were? God, Robyn, that's really racist."

He tried to roll his eyes, but they only bobbed up, showing yellow whites, and then dropped down. "Do you want the dress or not?"

"I want it, I want it."

Robyn motioned for her to lay her head on the bed again. Julie felt his fingertips lightly drum on her scalp. It was the same rhythm he'd been at since she'd arrived. She relaxed and shut her eyes to concentrate, thinking she'd never get it, they liked such different music. And yet, this beat felt familiar.

Robyn began humming, slightly off key, slightly breathless. Suddenly, she remembered a song Sister Hyacinth had taught everyone in the first grade. They'd had to sing it every morning before catechism. Robyn used to imitate her sweet shaky voice, later going sultry and batting his lashes.

Now Julie started to sing the words softly into the sheets and Robyn joined her: *"God loves me and I am special. I am one of God's bright stars. We are all God's special children. God loves us all, as we are."*

THE REVENGE OF CHUNKY BEEF

EMILY A. LEVY

I knew my family would be having thanksgiving dinner without me again. They do it every year now, ever since I became a lesbian. And ever since I came out to my mother, six years ago today, and told her some things about lesbians that she didn't want to know, she's basted her turkey with a spoon.

As far as they know, I'm not celebrating thanksgiving. Between my politics and my vegetarianism, it's not my favorite holiday. I've always made sure my family knows that. I'm the family troublemaker, the one who always talks about my reasons for being a vegetarian when everyone else is eating steak and I'm cramming my mouth with mashed potatoes and no gravy. I used to think there might be hope for Joanne, one of my little sisters, to reject that old american standard of animal genocide. But she took a lifelong vow of carnivorousness after she had the pleasure of seeing my parents' wrath leveled at me.

163

My folks think of me as stodgy, in a weird way. Tease me about how predictable I am, and how they count on me to complain about every racist remark they make. And, yes, certainly I ask them why they bother making those remarks, if they know they're racist. That's exactly the kind of moment when my parents show off their uncanny ability to light cigarettes in unison.

I refuse to be entirely predictable, though. This year I'm *celebrating* thanksgiving. Not in the traditional way, to be sure. But who knows? If my plans are successful, maybe this sort of celebration will become a tradition in my little subculture.

I have lit the candles on my altar. A yellow one for clarity, a lavender one to summon the supportive energies of my sisters, a black one for defiance, and a magenta for revenge. They sit on my altar surrounding my amethyst sphere, the stone I think of as representing my adult self which contains all of my child selves, as there are an infinite number of smaller spheres contained in every large one. The image of the sphere is an important one for me to keep with me today.

Lil and Rockwomon (keep your teeth in, it's a nickname) arrive with the costumes, and we have a fine time dressing up. Rockwomon is to be a clown, and we overdo the greasepaint smile on her to the point where we have very little room left on her face for the traditional red circles on the cheeks. Lil is a witch, because we couldn't resist. Pointy black hat, green rubber hands, stick-on wart, the works.

I am a can of campbell's soup. The real reason is that it's important to disguise my size and shape, but it could be said that I symbolize the children of america. In case you're interested, I am Chunky Beef. Lil and Rockwomb have practiced calling me "C.B." for a week, so they won't slip and call me Carla. My answering machine is totally confused.

Fifty balloons rest solidly on the ceiling, reminding us that we are celebrating. I've snuck one black one and a lavender in with the bunch of generic cheery brights. I have to have my symbols everywhere.

A xeroxed message dangles from the string of each balloon. I'm still uneasy about this part of the plan. What if the wind is so strong that the balloons land in a neighborhood where no one even *knows* my father? On the other hand, what if my mother's friends find them on their front lawns? Is that *really* what I want? Lil assures me that we can decide whether or not to release the balloons at the last minute.

It's time for a final run-through. Lil gives us the cue on her kazoo, and now that we are in costume we realize we've mixed our metaphors. If a kazoo is going to be played, it's the clown and not the witch who has to do it. Out of team spirit Rocky does not complain. Still, I know she cringes every time anyone even *refers* to a kazoo as a musical instrument. Rockwomon plays classical piano. (Years ago, Rachael refused the nickname "Rachmaninov," not wanting to be named after a man. We joked about calling her "Rock, Womon of" instead. The name — and all its derivatives — stuck.)

The kazoo hurdle safely jumped, we find our performance is ready. Rockwomon briefly complains that my nasal humming sounds more like creamed celery soup than chunky beef. What can I say?

I grab a sack of tofu jerky and a bottle of pomegranate juice and we pile into my toyota. Lil has to drive because the bottom rim of my can gets hitched up around my waist when I sit, and there's no way I'll fit behind the wheel.

The holiday crowds have thinned; the clear roads tell us that everyone's in their houses eating, or watching football, or beating each other up. Even the highway traffic isn't bad.

165

We pass a cop with a guy trying to walk a straight line. I want to take a picture of him and send it to the newspaper. I get like this when I go to the suburbs.

Lil, ever the amateur therapist, says I'm being cynical to cover up my fear, and that reminds me where we're going. Okay, so maybe she's right. But if somewhere inside me there's anywhere near as much fear as there is cynicism, it's a wonder I have any fingernails left at all. I prefer cynicism to fear, I prefer anger to fear, I prefer just about anything to fear. Do you blame me? So far, I prefer revenge to fear. I wonder for a moment what the relationship is between cynicism and revenge, and make a mental note to think about it later.

Lil slows down when I point out the house, but I urge her to keep going. I don't want my car to be recognized. We drive a couple blocks more, turn the corner, and park. My heart is pounding, "CHUNky-beef, CHUNky-beef, CHUNky-beef."

"Okay," I tell them, "our timing is perfect. I noticed the dining room light is on, so it's for sure they're eating." It's almost uncanny (pun intended) how well I know my mother and how distant I feel from her at the same time. As if keeping the light off in the dining room makes her annual holiday table setting a surprise. Shit, I think, maybe unveiling the table that way is her only hope of getting any attention for all the work she does preparing, and I start remembering how she'd spend two days in the kitchen before a holiday like this ... The thought of her basting the turkey the old way, before she knew about donor insemination, brings me back out of my little fantasy. No time to feel sorry for her now. CHUNky-beef, CHUNky-beef.

"Shit, we forgot the balloons!" I realize.

"You put them in the trunk," says Rocky. "You okay, C.B.?"

166

Lil reaches over and pats my hand, which I'm resting on the back of the front seat, between my two pals. "It's not too late to back out," she says.

Somehow I find that ironic. Three dykes in costume in the suburbs on turksgiving. Haven't we already crossed the line? I shake my head no.

"Believe me, we've got you covered." Lil shows me a small package wrapped in heavy brown paper. "We're prepared for anything."

"What's that?"

"Insurance," she says smugly, and tucks it back into her pocket.

"You two are the best," I say, "the absolute best. Thanks." I pat Lil's hand, and lean over to kiss Rockwoman. I knock her in the ear with my top rim instead.

Lil and Rock help me climb out of the car. They manage to get the top of my can hitched up over my head and unroll the round piece of fabric that's to become my lid. I pull my arms inside my costume; Lil velcroes the armholes shut. I thank her again for this ingenious design. Dykes are truly amazing.

Rockwoman and Lil have to lead me down the street, which is tricky since my love handles aren't available to hang onto. I can see through the fabric just fine in a lighted room, because my face is positioned real close to the cloth. Here, though, the street light doesn't suffice.

As we're walking up the block, witch and clown each with a bunch of balloons in one hand and the other on my can, I hope to hell the whole neighborhood is eating turkey right now. Sorry, turkeys, but I'm feeling entirely vulnerable. It's hard to believe that no one can see through my costume from the outside. It feels like anyone who looked could see all the way through to my brain, could know exactly what I have planned for the evening. Like when I first thought I might be a lesbian and was sure everyone could tell by looking at me.

We make our way up the driveway. Rockwomon informs me that another car has joined the lineup since we
cruised by a little while ago. The navy fiat she describes
belongs to my older brother Jim and his pregnant spouse.
Late, as usual. Jim and Denise have the classic "strong,
gentle man and frail, shy woman" relationship. Lil hands the
clown her balloons.

Lil rings the bell. CHUNky-beef, CHUNky-beef,
CHUNky-beef. Shit. Am I really going to do this? Someone
turns on the porch and driveway lights. I want to hang on
tight to my friends, but my hands can't reach much besides
the pockets of my 501s. At least now I can see.

Joanne answers the door. She's sixteen. Told me last
month that she mentally packs her suitcases for college
every night before she falls asleep. She's a sweetheart,
Joanne. I wish she didn't have to be here to see this.

Rocky and Lil are on the ball. The minute the door
opens, Rockwomon says, "A Cappella-Gram," and Lil puts
her finger to her smiling lips, hushing Joanne into com-
plicity. It works. Joanne stifles a giggle and leads us to the
dining room.

The whole family looks up from their meal. Dad faces us
from the head of the table. He's clearly annoyed at what
must certainly be a horde of filthy anarchists — who else
would dare interrupt the sanctity of the holiday? Mom's
hostess smile is only a little more tentative than usual as she
rises from her chair to greet whomever we might be. I can
see Jim trying not to look surprised as a witch, a clown, and
a giant soup can interrupt his dinner. Denise looks puzzled,
probably wondering if this is yet another Sims family tradition she's going to have to get used to. And Kat, home from
college, smiles broadly, ready to welcome this promise of
gaiety into her already-enchanted family.

Rockwomon fishes the kazoo out of her clown-sized
pocket and toots. She and Lil begin to sing. I hum along,

168

careful to remember the nasal tone that's part of my disguise.

oh, give me a home
with a pushbutton phone
where neighbors and siblings all play
where seldom is heard
a discouraging word
because everyone's happy all day.

home, home with the range
where a turkey is cooking away
where you can be assured
we were sent by a bird
your thanksgiving feast to delay.

I take a breath between chorus and verse to look around. They're all smiling now. Dad has pushed his chair back and folded his hands across his belly. His elbows rest on the arms of his chair. Mom has turned her chair a bit so she has a better view. Jim's trying to figure out who ordered this treat. No one is eating.

where the air is so pure
and the ladies demure
where faces are freckled and white
on this suburban street
secrets are not all sweet
we're here to uproot some tonight.

home, home can be strange
when families are not who they claim
the facade may be nice
but the kids pay the price
when they grow up with hearts full of shame.

I see confusion on their faces. I hear a little gasp, then a sniffle. I feel tears running down the side of my nose. I must really be out of my body — I had no idea that sniffle was me. I'm thankful to have this soup can to hide in. Somehow I manage to continue.

> *you can all be sure*
> *that this literature*
> *comes direct from your own dusty shelf*
> *our song was composed*
> *by whom you suppose*
> *if she could, she would be here herself.*

> *from home, she feels estranged*
> *it's at Dad we aim our exposé*
> *Martin Sims, you have erred*
> *your fate now is assured*
> *your fish we're about to fillet.*

The image makes me cringe. I swear I'm shaking. I can barely hear Rocky and Lil. I feel like it's only me up here. My stomach is churning. If I really were a can of soup, I'd have botulism by now for sure.

Somehow I manage to look out at them through both my emotional haze and the muslin one. Everyone's sitting up straight now. Only the Simses' resident "Cheshire Kat" still smiles. Could she really think we're singing about fish fillets? Maybe she could. Dad looks scared to death. I can see struggle on his face. Should he take this seriously? Is he really in trouble? Couldn't be. It's only some silly women in costume. Ha. He lights a cigarette. Sure enough, Mom is lighting one, too. Nothing to do but hum.

> *how often at night*
> *did your morals take flight*

170

and your toes tip to Carla's bedside
your sexual assaults
were not Carla's fault
and the truth she can no longer hide.

Dad's out of his chair, starting toward us. Shit. I knew I'd made the fucking song too long. Now what do we do? I look over at Rockwomon.

But it's Lil who takes action first. Suddenly she's cackling, raising her arms and pointing both green, knobby fore-fingers at Dad. Steam rises from her hips and nearly engulfs her face. "Halt!" she screeches. Everything freezes except Kat's smile, which falls to the floor.

Rockwomon begins to sing:

this home, home needs to change
a process we hope will ensue
we wish you no harm
as we sound this alarm
we'll leave now, without further ado.

Rocky turns and heads for the door, pausing only long enough to let one balloon fly to the ceiling, its tag fluttering. Lil grabs a handful of my costume and pulls me. I hear a rip. I don't care. We're smokin', headed for the door and out. "Slam it!" I whisper, and Lil obliges. I hear bits of dry ice fall from her pocket as she runs.

When we're halfway down the drive, I hear the door open. This is it. I know it. We're done for.

"Wait!" we hear. There's no way in hell.

But Lil stops and turns. I could kill her.

"It's Joanne," she says.

Joanne is pulling her coat on as she runs toward us. "I'm coming with you guys. Wait, okay? You *gotta* let me!"

"I don't know..." says Rockwomon.

171

"You sure?" asks Lil. "How come?"

"You've gotta take me to Carla," says Joanne, who has caught up with us by now. "Me and her have to talk."

Rocky unleashes the balloons.

THE CONTRIBUTORS

Shelley Anderson is a journalist who likes fiction because it's more real. Her short stories have appeared in U.S. and British anthologies, and she is finishing her first novel. She wants her mother to know that "One Sunday Morning" is only partly auto-biographical.

Elaine Auerbach was raised in Nutley, New Jersey, and moved to Canada in 1975. She now resides with the love of her life in Waterloo, Ontario. Her stories, poems, and articles have appeared in several journals and anthologies, including *Malahat Review, Dandelion, Dykewords,* and *Lesbian Bedtime Stories* 2. "Unan-nounced" is lovingly dedicated to Vandy (E.M.A.V) and to the women-loving women of the cedars.

Karen Barber lives in the Boston area with her lover, Susan, and their two cats. "A Date with Deth" is her first story. And probably her last.

Lucy Jane Bledsoe has turned from basketball to cycling, but she still considers the locker room to be fertile ground for good fiction. She has won the NEA/PEN Syndicated Fiction Project Award and a Money for Women/Barbara Deming Memorial Fund grant, and her short stories have appeared in several anthologies and journals. Lucy also writes novels and textbooks for New Adult Learners and teaches creative writing.

Jayne Relaford Brown performs poetry, teaches composition and women's writing workshops, and is a graduate student in creative writing at San Diego State University. This is her first published fiction. Her poetry has appeared in two anthologies, *Wanting Women: Erotic Lesbian Poetry* and *Silver-Tongued Sapphistry,* and several periodicals, including the *Minnesota Review.*

Ivy Burrowes is a writer and reviewer who lives in a cabin in the Rocky Mountains with her lover of twelve years, five cats, three dogs, and a totem pole. She earned a B.A. in English and history in 1985 from Metropolitan State College in Denver.

Nona Caspers's short stories have been collected in *Voyages Out 2,* co-authored by Julie Blackwomon. Her first novel, *The Blessed,* has just been published by Silverleaf Press.

Ouida Crozier was raised and educated in Florida, then lived for ten years in South Carolina, where she went to graduate school and came out to herself. Now a licensed psychologist with a part-time practice in Minnesota, Ouida works full-time as a computer programmer to support her practice and her writing and lives with a seventeen-year-old dog, the last of the canine companions of her youth.

Elissa Goldberg currently lives in Portland, Oregon, where she supports herself by working as a social worker in a nursing home. She has been writing short fiction for four years and is just beginning to publish her work. Soon to appear are two pieces in the anthologies *Riding Desire,* edited by Tee Corinne, and *Word of Mouth* 2, edited by Irene Zahava.

Pamela Gray is a poet, playwright, and screenwriter living in Los Angeles. Her work appears in several anthologies, including *New Lesbian Writing, Naming the Waves,* and *Cats and Their Dykes.* She co-parents an eight-year-old boy and dreams of selling a script and buying a house in the country.

Jessie Lynda Lasnover is a 42-year-old free-lance lesbian writer and mother of four whose work has been published in several journals and the anthology *Lesbian Bedtime Stories.* Formerly the assistant managing editor of the *Lesbian News,* she and her lover

174

live in California's San Joaquin Valley, where they have many animals, including one genuine attack rooster who is capable of making a grown man blanch and run.

Emily A. Levy works at the intersection of pain and humor, a street corner where she finds many other Jews. While her environmental illness prevents her from doing the political organizing she once lived for and many of the activities she used to enjoy, this disability has provided her a unique way to illustrate the damage humans are doing to the environment. This, her writing, and her commitment to children are her current ways of helping to create a world at peace.

Lee Lynch has written two books of short stories, *Old Dyke Tales* and *Home in Your Hands*. Her most recent novel is *That Old Studebaker*, released by Naiad Press in 1991. She writes a nationally syndicated column, "The Amazon Trail," from her home in rural Oregon.

Kathleen M. Quinlan is a Chicagoan who writes to learn what she knows. She has published fiction and poetry and is looking for a home for a children's novel. "Most of all," she writes, "I would love to meet everyone who reads my story. Let's do lunch!"

Carol Seajay is a white, working-class midwesterner who still believes in fixing cars with baling wire and bobby pins. She gave up life in the closeted Midwest twenty years ago for the queerer life in San Francisco. She co-founded Old Wives' Tales bookstore and now edits and publishes the *Feminist Bookstore News*. She writes, "You can laugh at my car, but I drive a *very* fast computer!"

Wickie Stamps is a forty-year-old novice writer and burnt-out political activist who refuses to succumb to her rage or her despair. As a means of survival she has been forced to develop a sense of humor about herself, her life, and her political work. For her, a good day is when she doesn't throttle some uppity thing in the movement — or choke on her own self-righteousness.

Karen Dale Wolman is a gay journalist and fiction writer. Over the past several years, she has written a column for *Nightlife* and contributed regularly to *Frontiers, The Advocate, Les Meet,* and the

Lesbian News. Her fiction has been published in several magazines and anthologies. The *National Enquirer* tried to recruit her once, but she told them what she thought of their ethics. They never called back.

Tina Portillo is a dyke of color who has spent several years on the staff of Alyson Publications. Her secret wish — which just came true — was to see her name on the cover of a book by the time she hit forty. Her passions are reading science fiction and fantasy, writing porn, riding with a Boston-based women's motorcycle club, and having hot leathersex.

Other books of interest from
ALYSON PUBLICATIONS

CRUSH, by Jane Futcher, $8.00. In her senior year at Huntington Hill, an exclusive girls' school, Jinx finally felt as if she belonged because beautiful, popular Lexie wanted her for a friend. Jinx knew she had a serious crush on Lexie, and knew she had to do something to make it go away. But Lexie, who always got her way, had other plans.

HAPPY ENDINGS ARE ALL ALIKE, by Sandra Scoppettone, $7.00. It was their last summer before college, and Jaret and Peggy were in love. But as Jaret said, "It always seems as if when something great happens, then something lousy happens soon after."

RAPTURE AND THE SECOND COMING, by Wendy Borgstrom, $8.00. Gwen is running from a failed but passionate first romance with an alcoholic. She lands in New York City where she buries her anger by acting out *all* her sexual fantasies.

TRAVELS WITH DIANA HUNTER, by Regine Sands, $8.00. When eighteen-year-old Diana Hunter runs away from her hometown of Lubbock, Texas, she begins an unparalleled odyssey of love, lust, and humor that spans almost twenty years.

ALARMING HEAT, by Regine Sands, $8.00. The author of the popular *Travels with Diana Hunter* is back with more tales of lesbian erotic adventure. *Alarming Heat* aims to please, and with something for everyone, it does.

THE RAGING PEACE, by Artemis OakGrove, $8.00. The love achieved by Leslie, a lawyer, and Ryan, a skilled pilot, is threatened by the thirst for revenge of a powerful, centuries-old goddess named Anara.

DREAMS OF VENGEANCE, by Artemis OakGrove, $8.00. Leslie and Ryan's love is tested again by the goddess Anara who manipulates their sex slaves, Sanji and Corelle. The two lovers test the bounds of power and desire in ritualized, passionate sex.

THRONE OF COUNCIL, by Artemis OakGrove, $8.00. Ryan and Leslie face a final battle against Anara, high priestess and demi-goddess who seeks their deaths and the title of Queen Regent of the Throne.

BETWEEN FRIENDS, by Gillian E. Hanscombe, $8.00. The four women in this book represent different outlooks, yet are tied together by the bonds of friendship. Through their experiences, Hanscombe shows the close relationship between politics and everyday lives.

TESTIMONIES, edited by Sarah Holmes, $8.00. Twenty-two lesbians of widely varying backgrounds and ages give accounts of their journeys toward self-discovery.

THE ALYSON ALMANAC, by Alyson Publications, $9.00. Gay and lesbian history and biographies, scores of useful addresses and phone numbers, and much more, are all gathered in this useful yet entertaining reference.

BI ANY OTHER NAME, edited by Loraine Hutchins and Lani Kaahumanu, $12.00. In this ground-breaking anthology, hear the voices of over seventy women and men from all walks of life describe their lives as bisexuals in prose, poetry, art, and essays.

CHOICES, by Nancy Toder, $8.00. In this straightforward, sensitive novel, Nancy Toder conveys the fear and confusion of a woman coming to terms with her attraction to other women.

LAVENDER LISTS, by Lynne Y. Fletcher and Adrien Saks, $9.00. *Lavender Lists* starts where *The Gay Book of Lists* and *Lesbian Lists* left off! Dozens of clever and original lists give you interesting and entertaining snippets of gay and lesbian lore.

LESBIAN LISTS, by Dell Richards, $9.00. Fun facts like banned lesbian books, lesbians who've passed as men, black lesbian entertainers, and switch-hitters are sure to amuse and make *Lesbian Lists* a great gift.

WORLDS APART, edited by Camilla Decarnin, Eric Garber, Lyn Paleo, $8.00. The world of science fiction allows writers to freely explore alternative sexualities. These eleven stories take full advantage of that opportunity as they voyage into the futures that could await us. The authors of these stories explore issues of sexuality and gender relations in the context of futuristic societies. *Worlds Apart* challenges us by showing us our alternatives.

A MISTRESS MODERATELY FAIR, by Katherine Sturtevant, $9.00. An entertaining and well-researched historical romance about two women — one a playwright, the other an actress — in Shakespearean England. This is the first lesbian novel set in the Restoration.

UNBROKEN TIES, by Carol S. Becker, $8.00. Through a series of personal accounts and interviews, Dr. Carol Becker, a practicing psychotherapist, charts the various stages of lesbian breakups and examines the ways women maintain relationships with their ex-lovers.

GLORIA GOES TO GAY PRIDE, by Lesléa Newman; illustrated by Russell Crocker, $8.00. Gay Pride Day is fun for Gloria, and for her two mothers. Here, the author of *Heather Has Two Mommies* describes the special day from the viewpoint of a young girl. Ages 3–7.

HOW WOULD YOU FEEL IF YOUR DAD WAS GAY?, by Ann Heron and Meredith Maran; illustrated by Kris Kovick, cloth, $10.00. When Jasmine announces in class that her dad is gay, her brother complains that she had no right to reveal a fact that he wanted to keep secret. This, and other concerns facing the children of lesbian and gay parents, are addressed in the context of real-life situations. Ages 8–12.

FAMILIES, by Michael Willhoite, $3.00. Many kinds of families, representing a diversity of races, generations, and cultural backgrounds, as well as gay and lesbian parents, are depicted in this coloring book. Ages 2–6.

LONG TIME PASSING, edited by Marcy Adelman, $8.00. Older lesbians tell of their lives, loves, and of the building of a sense of community.

SUPPORT YOUR LOCAL BOOKSTORE

Most of the books described above are available at your nearest gay or feminist bookstore, and many of them will be available at other bookstores. If you can't get these books locally, order by mail using the form below.

Enclosed is $_____ for the following books. (Add $1.00 postage when ordering just one book. If you order two or more, we'll pay the postage.)

1. _____

2. _____

3. _____

name: _____

address: _____

city: _____ state: _____ zip: _____

ALYSON PUBLICATIONS
Dept. H-95, 40 Plympton St., Boston, MA 02118

After December 31, 1992, please write for current catalog.